S

D1102532

Tsire Mushoma

The Bridesmaid's Lover

SAPPHIRE PRESS

Sapphire Press is the romance imprint of Kwela Books,
an imprint of NB Publishers,
40 Heerengracht, Cape Town, South Africa
PO Box 6525, Roggebaai, 8012, South Africa
sapphire@kwela.com

Copyright © T Mushoma 2010

Cover image by Gallo Images/Getty Images
Cover design by Hanneke du Toit
Typography by Nielfa Cassiem-Carelse
Set in Plantin
Printed and bound by Ultra Litho, Johannesburg,
South Africa

First edition, first impression 2010

ISBN: 978-0-7957-0303-4

For my mom,
for being my greatest inspiration,
pillar of strength and for always knowing
what looks good on me

1

Zandi Zungu put on the coral dress and a pair of silver heels. Although she had fitted the dress at the shop just an hour ago, she'd had bad experiences in the past with shop mirrors being misleading. But even before she tried on the dress for the second time, she doubted that it would look any less beautiful on her than it had an hour ago. In fact, staring at her reflection in the mirror now, she decided it flattered her even more than she had thought at the shop.

She liked how the ruffles transformed her boyish figure by giving an illusion of feminine curves. The V-shaped neckline flattered her small bust and the sleeveless cut showed off her beautiful shoulders. The dress went down all the way to her calves in a draping of ruffles, showing off her long, lean legs through them. This is the perfect dress, Zandi thought to herself. No wonder it took me so long to find it.

If only finding a date was like finding a dress. But that was proving to be much more challenging than she had imagined. Her thoughts drifted to Jeffrey and how easy things would have been if he were still around. But he was gone and she was constantly feeling as if she had to start all over again, rebuilding her life from the very beginning. She had planned a lot of things around her and Jeffrey, and that made it more difficult to get over him.

Zandi decided thinking about her ex didn't do her any good, so she focused on the dress again. She hadn't noticed it initially, but its colour looked so much brighter in contrast to her almost caramel complexion. She twisted her braids in her hand and piled them up on top of her head. She decided that wearing her hair up would work better for the dress; that would also show off her well-defined cheekbones. And she would apply almost no make-up, thereby emphasising her full lips and naturally long eyelashes.

At the sound of the doorbell, Zandi quickly slipped out of the dress and the shoes and into a pair of slippers and a dressing gown which she tied on her way to the door. She was expecting her friends Neo Ledwaba and Tondani Munyai, and from the insistent way the bell was ringing she just knew that it was them.

"Okay, okay! Here I am. Or are you trying to break my doorbell?"

"No, we were trying to break down your door. You can't call and say you have an emergency, only to leave us stranded at the door for ten minutes," Tondani answered, glancing at her watch.

Tondani was almost the same height as Zandi but she was curvier. She looked glamorous in a purple floral wrap dress and a pair of plum heels. Zandi envied her friend the way her make-up always looked perfect, regardless of the time of day. She also had what Zandi thought was the perfect canvas for make-up: a flawless skin. Tondani had bright eyes that never looked reddish at the end of the day, perfect white teeth, thanks to her cosmetic dentist, and perfectly shaped eyebrows. Her weave danced around her face in a silken curtain of soft curls.

"Oh, please, it wasn't that long! Come on in and I'll pour you some juice." Zandi led the two ladies into the lounge.

"Just juice? I'm sorry, but I need something stronger for what you've just put me through. I was starting to think that something bad had happened to you." Neo fanned her face with her hand as if she was under tremendous stress.

Neo Ledwaba was the shortest of the three women. She had a short weave that was curled outwards all around, framing her sweet-looking face. She had small eyes, but her friends always joked that they never missed a thing. The only make-up Neo wore was clear lip gloss. Compared to Tondani, she looked casual in blue jeans, a black T-shirt and flat black sandals.

"Neo, you're such a drama queen. I don't keep alcohol in the house; you know how it goes when I'm feeling depressed. The juice is really good." Zandi disappeared into the kitchen and reappeared a few minutes later with three glasses of juice on a round tray.

Zandi's lounge was a rectangular open-plan living space that comprised both a sitting and a dining area. There was an archway that led into a passage that in turn led to the kitchen, bathroom and two bedrooms. At one end of the lounge there was a rectangular dark-wood dining table with six matching chairs which formed the dining area. The sitting area had a long dark-brown couch, a four-seater that Zandi thought was the most comfortable couch she had ever sat on. In front of the couch was a glass coffee table, and then there was a long cabinet that Zandi used as a TV stand and a bookshelf. The cushions that were scattered liberally on the couch provided colour in the room.

"So what is this emergency that you had to pull me out of work for? Do you know how busy I am this week?" Tondani took a sip of juice as she eagerly waited for the answer.

Zandi was enjoying the moment, sipping her juice slowly, clearly in no hurry to tell her friends why she had asked them to come past her house.

"What I want to know is why you're looking so . . . happy. Whatever you mixed into your juice, I want it. You were all sad and depressed yesterday; now look at you!" Neo added.

"You make it sound as if being happy is a crime," Tondani reproached her. "The girl deserves some happiness."

"I just want to know her secret . . . Do you have any idea how much this wedding is stressing me out? Hmm . . . this stuff tastes nice." Neo had raised her glass and was looking at it as if she wanted to see why the juice tasted good.

"You know my answer to stress: retail therapy. Especially when you find the perfect bridesmaid's dress," Zandi finally confessed, beaming at the thought that she had found it all on her own.

"You went to look for the dress without us?" Tondani looked genuinely shocked, as if she had just heard about something happening that she had always thought was impossible.

"I didn't go looking for the dress. I was just out clearing my head at lunchtime when I saw it. I almost walked right past that shop! I'm glad I didn't, though, because when I tried it on there was no doubt in my mind that I'd found the perfect dress. So I went back there after work and bought it," Zandi said excitedly.

"I can't believe you bought something without us seeing it first! Never mind, we'll be returning that dress if it isn't good enough. Go ahead then, we want to see it." Tondani gave Zandi a slight push from the couch.

"Okay, ladies, get ready to be dazzled!"

Zandi disappeared into her room and closed the door behind her. When she reappeared, she had changed back into the dress. She walked along the length of the lounge, pretending to be on a catwalk and twirling at each end to show off the ruffles.

"Aren't you going to say anything? Do I look that bad in it?"

"Uhm . . . I suppose we're just lost for words. It looks amazing on you. We've been looking for this outfit every-where; where has it been?" Tondani stood up so that she could see the dress properly.

"Oh no, I'm not lost for words. I can't let you come to my wedding looking that beautiful! All eyes are supposed to be on the bride, and that's me," Neo gasped between large sips of juice.

Tondani went to sit next to Neo. Putting her arm around her friend, she gave her a squeeze. "The bride shouldn't worry, because as your bridesmaid I will make sure that you are the fairest of them all. As for you, my friend, this dress fits you nicely."

"That's a relief! I couldn't handle parting with it if you wanted me to return it. Getting a nod from the fashion editor is always good. But wait, there's more!" Zandi quickly went back to her room.

"As if you don't look beautiful enough already!" Neo called after her. "You'll have to forgive me if I replace you as bridesmaid."

Zandi reappeared holding a black suit, a white shirt with coral stripes and a coral tie. She held the clothes up for her friends to see.

Tondani was confused. "Is that a man's suit?"

"Please don't wear that to my wedding!" pleaded Neo.

"It's not for me, but look at how the tie matches my dress. And the tie goes really well with this shirt, so I couldn't *not* buy both. And then there was the suit. Doesn't everything just go together so well?"

Tondani was still confused. "Sure, but I still don't understand why you'd buy men's clothes when you look this good in this dress?"

"It's for my date, silly. If I'm going to be looking this gorgeous, then my date also needs to look the part, don't you agree?"

Neo wondered if she had missed something while focusing on the juice she was drinking. "But I thought you didn't have a date for the wedding?"

"I don't have one *yet*, but the wedding is still two months away. That's plenty of time to charm a man into being my date, right?"

"I totally agree, except I don't know how you can buy a

suit for a man you haven't met yet. What if you do meet him, and he's too skinny or too fat or too tall?" Tondani couldn't understand what had gotten into Zandi.

"I'm not thinking about that right now; you're the one who told me to forget about the what-ifs. All I know is that my date and I will make a great couple in these outfits. Just make sure your photographer friend shows up, because this is the stuff the fashion society pages are made of." Zandi had it all figured out. She had found a dress she looked amazing in. She had also found an elegant suit that went perfectly with her dress. How could she possibly not find a man to wear it and be her date for the wedding when everything else had worked out so perfectly?

"I bet you bought the suit with Jeffrey in mind. Look at it; it's his size!" Neo had emptied her glass of juice and now moved on to sipping Zandi's juice, which had hardly been touched.

"What?" was all Zandi managed to say, so shocked was she by her friend's suggestion.

"I'm simply saying maybe you should ask Jeffrey to be your date."

Tondani looked a little shocked at how Neo had just brought up his name. "I disagree. How can you waste a suit like that on him? No way!"

"And quite honestly, Jeffrey hates suits. He would never wear this!" Zandi concurred.

"I was just making a suggestion. Maybe as a last resort, just in case," Neo persisted.

"How could I ever ask Jeffrey? After what he did to me?"

"Forget about him; we'll find you a date for the wedding and he won't be a lowlife like Jeffrey," Tondani tried to resolve the situation before it got worse.

"I thought you were the one who broke up with him?" Neo blinked innocently as Tondani shot a warning glance her way.

"Well, I did," replied Zandi, close to tears. "What else was I supposed to have done when the guy I'd been with for five years told me he wasn't ready for commitment?"

"You did the right thing. Jeffrey didn't deserve you. Neo, please pass some tissues," asked Tondani, giving Neo a see-what-you've-done look.

"Anyway, what did he mean, he wasn't ready for commitment?" Zandi asked as she started to sob. "Am I controlling? Is that what he meant?"

Tondani rescued the suit from Zandi and placed it neatly on the couch so that her friend would not damage it by sobbing all over it.

"You know what? It doesn't matter," Neo tried to console Zandi. "Whatever he meant, it's really not important any more. Don't cry; you're going to ruin that beautiful dress."

Zandi gasped as her attention turned to the outfit she was still wearing, but then she seemed to decide that it didn't matter any more because she started to cry again. "He's ruined everything, absolutely everything. How could he be so cruel?"

"Jeffrey has always been like that," Neo retorted. "That's why I never really liked him."

"So why do you insist that she comes to your wedding with him?" Tondani asked Neo.

"Remember the time we all went to the festival in Mafikeng? It was five of us: you and Lutendo, Zandi and Jeffrey, and I was alone. I was the only girl who didn't have a boyfriend. Remember what Jeffrey said to me? He said he didn't think I was anywhere close to finding a man. That's why it would be great for me to have him there when I get married, just to see the look on his cruel face."

Tondani sighed at Neo's explanation. "Don't mind her; the wedding is stressing her out," she said.

But that didn't make Zandi feel better. "I'm alone because I'm clingy and controlling. Look at me, buying a suit for a man I haven't even met yet. What's the matter with me?"

Zandi didn't want to think about the wedding gown that was in her closet. She wondered if she would ever get to wear it. Why had she even bought something like that with no marriage proposal in sight?

"It means you are in control, which isn't the same thing as being controlling," Tondani said and then continued, "Say you meet a handsome man a day before the wedding and he doesn't own a suit? That would be disastrous, so I think it's good that you take charge like this; it's very sexy."

Zandi managed a laugh and started to dry her eyes with a tissue.

"You'll be okay, girlfriend. You'll find a date for the wedding, and in time you'll find a really wonderful man who has eyes only for you. Uhm . . . you know my brother has always liked you," Tondani joked.

"Is he still single?" Neo asked. "I'm surprised, because you market him any chance you get. I remember you said exactly the same about your brother to me before I met Thabo."

"I did? It just bothers me that he always goes for the wrong type of girls and they always break his heart. He's a real sweetheart." Tondani looked affectionately at Zandi, who raised both hands.

"No offence, but I'm not that desperate. Your brother isn't my type."

"Don't give up, Zandi. I'd already given up all hope of finding a good man worth spending the rest of my life with when Thabo came along and swept me off my feet." Neo could hardly hide how happy she was.

"I thought you just stalked the poor guy," Zandi said.

"Oh well, sometimes you need to haunt them until they realise they can't live without you. If you decide to go that route, I'm here should you need advice."

"You know, you are unbelievable sometimes. Anyway, we really need to get going. How about we meet for lunch tomorrow?" Tondani was already getting up from the couch.

Zandi thought lunch with friends might be just what she needed to get her mind off work and Jeffrey, even if it was just for a short while. "Lunch would be great."

"I'm not sure I can get away from work," Neo mumbled.

"Yes, you can, and it's essential that you do. You spend the whole day with five-year-olds; you need a break for some intelligent conversation with grown-ups. I'll fetch you on my way. Zandi, sleep well and please don't think about people who make you sad." Tondani rubbed her friend's shoulder as they walked to the door.

Zandi wished they didn't have to leave. She loved that she could talk and laugh – and sometimes cry – with people who truly understood her. Being alone made her sad most of the time.

"Thanks for coming over. I really appreciate it."

Zandi had closed the door and was just about to go and change clothes when her brother Sizwe walked into the lounge.

"Wow! Are you going somewhere?"

"No, I'm not. This is the dress I'm wearing to Neo's wedding. I was just trying it on."

"It's pretty and it suits you." Sizwe smiled shyly at Zandi.

"Thanks." Zandi smiled back at her brother, then picked up the suit from the couch and went to her room.

After she had changed, she hung both the dress and the suit in her closet. Looking at the suit, she could imagine her date in it, more handsome than ever. At the end of the day he would take off the jacket and look dashing in the white shirt. Zandi couldn't help it, but she just had to imagine this irresistible man in her kitchen, cooking them dinner. But at that moment she heard Sizwe calling from the kitchen, asking about dinner, and so she was brought back to reality.

There was no dashing man in her kitchen.

2

Zandi had worked as an economist for Modise & Associates since graduating from Wits University, and she still enjoyed her job as much as she did when she started there five years ago. Modise & Associates was a consulting firm which had been started by an old man everyone affectionately referred to as Modise. Although it was a small company, it had been in existence for over thirty years and employed people who had years of experience in the finance industry and were good at their jobs. Zandi had chosen to work for a smaller firm because she felt it would allow her to grow as an individual, while feeling appreciated as an important member of the team.

She had started at Modise & Associates as an eager graduate, wanting to learn everything she needed to know in order to do her job well. It had been a wonderful opportunity to have Modise as her manager and mentor. Zandi always thought he was the most patient man she knew. She admired his wisdom and intelligence, and was grateful that he was always happy to share everything he knew about the business. She was aware that Modise had high expectations of her, and in turn she worked hard to prove to him just how committed she was to growing as an expert in her field of work.

Before Sizwe came to stay with her at her flat in Fourways, a twelve-hour workday was standard for Zandi, especially after she broke up with Jeffrey. Spending most of the day at the office was the only thing that kept her from breaking every single thing in her flat; she was too exhausted by the time she got home at night. Eventually the anger had subsided and loneliness took its place. She hated coming back to an empty place after a long day at work. Although she and Jeffrey had not lived together, he had spent a lot of time at her flat and she had never known what it felt like to be alone.

That was when she decided to ask her mother if her brother could come and stay with her. It was an arrangement that Zandi felt could benefit both him and her. She needed the company and Sizwe would be able to go to a better school in the city. Like him, she had also gone to school in Nongoma, a small village in KwaZulu-Natal. Siyaphakama High School, like most rural schools, didn't have many facilities beyond tables and chairs. The teachers did their best with the little they had to work with, but Zandi still remembered how difficult it was for her when she started at Wits University. She had to work twice as hard just to have the same level of understanding of the work as the other students who had gone to schools in town. For that reason she felt things could be easier for Sizwe if he came to stay with her.

Zandi thought her brother had settled in well at Fourways High. He had been more excited than nervous at the thought of starting at a new school in a completely different place. What worried Zandi was that her mother didn't have any other children besides her and Sizwe and would now be left at home alone. Zandi believed it when her mom assured her that she could manage on her own, but still worried about her. On some days Zandi worried about her brother too. Although he had taken the move well, she had never lived with a teenage boy before and didn't know how to look after one.

Although Sizwe was well mannered and never caused any trouble, Zandi couldn't help but worry about the influence the big city might have on a boy who'd spent all his life in a small village. Her mother had done a wonderful job of raising Sizwe and she didn't want to undo the discipline instilled in him. There were times she felt overwhelmed, not knowing who his friends were or if he came straight home after school. Zandi dropped him off there on her way to work in the mornings, but he had to walk back to the flat in the afternoons.

She supervised his homework and then felt guilty that maybe she was being too strict with him, remembering that teenagers didn't like to feel as if they were being kept on a tight leash all the time. Even though mostly she felt she had no idea of what was required of her, Zandi definitely didn't want to feel as if she wasn't trying hard enough. Long hours spent at work became a thing of the past; she made sure she came back in time to have supper with her brother. If needed, she worked at home in the evenings, after seeing to it that Sizwe had done his schoolwork.

Zandi was busy working on her laptop, happy that Sizwe had done his homework, when her house phone rang. She almost jumped; nobody phoned her at that time of the night, and she immediately thought of her mother alone in Nongoma.

"Hello?" she answered cautiously.

"Girl, what are you still doing up this late?"

Zandi was relieved to hear it was Tondani on the phone. "What are *you* doing? You always go to bed at eight." Tondani was the one person Zandi knew who could sleep the whole day and the whole night and not even complain of a headache on waking up.

"Not tonight. Lutendo invited some of his friends over for dinner and they've just left. I can feel it's long past my bedtime; I'm too old for late nights. But you didn't answer my question."

"I'm working," Zandi answered sheepishly. Tondani had made it clear that it wasn't healthy for Zandi to pour herself into work the way she did after her break-up. Zandi had promised to take her friend's advice and not take work home, but rather spend the evenings watching movies or reading a book that had nothing to do with the economy.

"Goodness, Zandi; I'm going to talk to Modise about this. The man is capitalising on you being single by making you work all the time! Single people also need some rest."

"Modise has nothing to do with it; I choose to work." Zandi really didn't feel like arguing.

"That's the problem. Your boss is loafing and you're doing all the work. Anyway, that's not why I called. I've got exciting news – I just couldn't wait until tomorrow to tell you! There's this guy – he's Lutendo's friend and his name is Rhulani Mhinga. He joined us for breakfast once at the festival in Mafikeng last year."

Zandi remembered the festival and she certainly remembered that she and Jeffrey had a lot of fun. But she definitely didn't recall having breakfast with a friend of Lutendo's. "No, I don't think I met him. Anyway, I only had eyes for Jeffrey back then."

"It's good to know that you weren't busy ogling some other guy."

"As if that mattered to Jeffrey." Zandi could feel the sad thoughts fighting to come to the surface. She had managed to keep them buried since the time she broke down in front of Neo and Tondani, and she didn't feel like crying herself to sleep tonight. So she quickly focused her thoughts on the cultural dances and other things she had seen and enjoyed at the festival.

"Why are we even talking about Jeffrey? So this Rhulani asked about you and was very interested when he heard that you were now single. He wants to meet you so bad that he tried to bribe me." Tondani lowered her voice to a whisper. "I accepted the bribe, so you can't say no."

"What? You just went ahead and told him that your single friend was desperate to find a boyfriend?"

"Not really; I simply mentioned it while everyone was still seated at the table. Just kidding, you know I have a way of putting things way nicer than that. The point is, he's *dying* to meet you, so it's up to you if you want to save the guy's life or not."

"Okay, did you give him my number?" Zandi knew the answer to the question even before hearing it. She was getting nervous just thinking about what Tondani had already told this guy about her.

"I did, and I made a reservation for dinner tomorrow evening."

"What?"

"Tomorrow evening you're going out on a date with Rhulani. Tell Modise it's his turn to work the night shift!"

"Tondani . . . I don't know . . ." The mere thought of going dating a man she hadn't even met properly made Zandi itch all over.

"You don't need to know anything. Just be there when he comes to pick you up. I said he should call you to get the directions to your place, but the truth is, I've already told him where you live."

"Are you trying to get me stalked?"

"If that's what it takes to get you off that couch. I hope you realise a piece of furniture doesn't count as a companion?"

"You're wicked!"

"Tell me, what are you wearing?"

"Why is that any of your business?"

"Are you in those peanut-sack pants again?"

Zandi looked at the brown tracksuit pants she was wearing and couldn't see anything wrong with them. "Come on, they're warm and comfortable."

"Meaning they look really ugly on you, or you look really ugly in them. Making each other look really ugly is not on.

Please find a way to get rid of those pants before they scare Rhulani away."

"He's never going to see me in them!" Zandi wasn't even sure she wanted to see the man at all.

"Oh, I like the way you speak," her friend joked. "So what *is* Rhulani going to see you in?"

"Tondani, please go to sleep!"

"You're right; I need to get off the phone before I'm served with divorce papers. Good night, and don't forget – hot date tomorrow night. You can thank me afterwards."

"Why do I have a feeling I'll never be thanking you, ever?"

"Because sometimes you can be an ungrateful thing! Sleep well."

"Good night, bye!"

Zandi put the phone down and immediately felt nervous about the date with Rhulani. She had told herself she was ready to start dating again, but she hadn't anticipated that it would happen so soon. And the fact that it was with someone she didn't know was making her even more scared. Tondani had just gone ahead and made all the arrangements without consulting her first. She'd imagined she would meet a guy and get to know him before going out on a date; that way she would at least know what she could talk to him about.

But now Zandi was supposed to get ready for an evening with a man whose hair colour she didn't even know. How did you prepare for such a date? Did you read all the daily newspapers to make sure you had something to say about what's going on in the world? If that was the case, she was in trouble, because she had not been following the news lately. She could confidently discuss movements in the markets and financial indicators, but she didn't think that was appropriate conversation for a date.

Maybe she needed to get an early night the evening before to make sure her mind was sharp and she could think on her feet. It would be a disaster if she couldn't even comment on the pollution in downtown Johannesburg.

Zandi decided that it was a good idea to get a decent night's rest, so she switched off her laptop and went to bed.

3

Zandi remembered the day she went for a job interview at Modise & Associates. She had been so nervous that she didn't even realise she was wearing shoes that didn't match until after arriving at the offices. On seeing that she just panicked even more, but Modise made a joke about it and somehow that made Zandi relax and focus on the interview. She had got the job, but Modise never forgot the incident with the shoes, and they sometimes still had a good laugh about it.

Thinking about what happened five years ago, Zandi realised she was once again feeling as if she was going for a job interview. The only difference was that she had the whole day to be nervous about her approaching date in the evening. She desperately hoped that there would not be another incident like the one with the shoes; she didn't think she would get over the embarrassment.

By the time she got to work in the morning, Zandi had already decided that she wasn't looking to start another relationship. She was just going to go out with this Rhulani and enjoy some dinner. Maybe he would become a good friend and then she could ask him to go to the wedding with her. He didn't need to be her boyfriend for that. But even with all these reassurances, Zandi couldn't help feeling like a teenager going on her first date. Sitting in her office, she kept looking at her watch and doing a countdown the way she always did before she had to do any public speaking.

At some point she hoped Rhulani had lost her number, or that he would change his mind about the date, or maybe catch flu or anything that would make him stay at home. Much to Zandi's dismay, he called her shortly after she had arrived at work. Then she knew there was no going back, and that scared her even more.

In contrast, Rhulani sounded very calm on the phone. It was as if they had made their plans for the date face to face and he was now just calling to confirm. That comforted Zandi a little; at least he didn't sound as if he regretted having agreed to this blind date.

Blind date! That's it; maybe that's why she was feeling so nervous. Zandi had never gone on one before and was convinced something like that could only end in disaster. It was horrible that her first date in five years with a different guy was a blind date, as if things couldn't get any worse!

For some reason the day seemed to go by too quickly, drawing her faster to this occasion she was dreading so much. Rhulani was supposed to pick her up at half past seven, and Zandi decided to leave work early to make sure she had more than enough time to get ready.

As she got dressed, she was feeling frustrated because she did not know what to wear on a first date. If only she had thought of asking Tondani to come and help her get ready; after all, she was the one who had got her into this situation. Zandi didn't want to look overdressed, but she also didn't want to look as if she hadn't made any effort at all.

After countless changes of clothes she settled on a little black number that she thought flattered her figure without looking too dressy. She added a pair of black pumps and silver stud earrings, and left her braids loose. All that was left now was to wait for Rhulani while her nerves played havoc with her.

As she waited, she mentally went through what she would do in case things didn't go well. Say Rhulani was her mother's age; she wouldn't want to be rude, so she would just pray for him to fall asleep before eight and then leave him at the restaurant. If he was younger than twenty-five, which she doubted would be the case since it was Tondani who had set them up, she would definitely stick around and see how it went. If he tried to grab her in any way, she had two cans of pepper spray: one in her handbag and another one strapped to her thigh. If he was a serial killer, she was armed with the emergency police number.

Just at that moment the doorbell rang and Zandi quickly double-checked that she had 10111 on speed dial before going to the front door.

"Hi!" she greeted the man at the door, immediately thinking that she'd spoken too loudly and therefore sounded overeager. However, she was relieved that he wasn't her mother's age. In fact, he seemed to be in his mid-thirties. Zandi couldn't help noticing his almond-shaped eyes that looked almost like a tiger's when he smiled – and what a seductive smile he had! He had good, dark skin that glowed beautifully. His hair and beard were trimmed short. He was only slightly taller than her and slightly bulky, but not too muscular. He looked smart in a formal green striped shirt and khaki chinos.

"Hi, you must be Zandi," Rhulani replied coolly, extending his hand to her. She was instantly charmed by his charismatic Eddie Zondi-like voice. There was something about Rhulani that captivated her. He was like a calm ocean, and yet she felt as if she was in the midst of rough seas where she was battling to keep steady.

She dropped her gaze to his arms. The shirtsleeves were rolled back a little, showing off the strong arms underneath. Zandi quickly returned her gaze to Rhulani's face; if she looked at those arms a second longer, she was afraid she would just fall over so that he could catch her.

"And you must be Rhulani. Nice to meet you." This time Zandi made sure to speak with a lowered voice and shook his hand without looking at his arms. She noted that his hands were warm; the kind she would enjoy holding all the time.

"Nice of you to agree to meet me." Rhulani said the words while still holding her hand, and then he slowly let it go.

Zandi was a little relieved; at least her heartbeat could now return to normal.

"I'll get my handbag," she said, then blushed and added awkwardly, "Sorry, I already have it."

Rhulani could see that Zandi was a little embarrassed and smiled at her.

"Shall we go then?" he asked and she nodded, closing the door behind them.

On the way to the restaurant Zandi felt uneasy about being in a strange man's car. Just because it was Tondani who had set them up didn't mean she could trust Rhulani – especially because Tondani was behind it all! Just because she thought he was such a handsome man didn't mean she could trust him either.

She regretted not suggesting that they take her car; she would have felt much safer, even if Rhulani was driving. At least she knew where all the tools were hidden, in case she needed to defend herself.

If he noticed how uneasy Zandi was, Rhulani didn't say anything, but he tried his best to make her feel comfortable by keeping her engaged in conversation.

Eventually they arrived at the restaurant and Zandi was relieved to be out in the open again.

The first thing she thought when they entered was that the atmosphere in the place was too romantic. The lights were dimmed and there were candles flickering on the tables. The music was too soft and everyone looked too cosy. It made her wonder if Tondani was friends with the manager of the restaurant.

Other than that, Zandi liked the African masks on the wall, the long reeds in large earthenware pots and the rough wood of the tables and chairs that gave everything a mysterious feel. She thought this was rather appropriate as the setting for her date with this man she knew so little about.

Rhulani and Zandi sat down at a corner table overlooking the lights of Sandton. She figured that if the date didn't turn out well, at least she would have enjoyed the view – of Sandton *and* of Rhulani.

"You look nervous," he said once they had ordered their food.

"I never thought going on a blind date would be this intimidating. But I can feel myself starting to relax, slowly," Zandi admitted.

"If it makes any difference, I've never been on a blind date before either. I am also feeling nervous deep down. I'm just trying to take it like a man and not let it show. That is, I hope it isn't showing," Rhulani joked and they both laughed. Zandi was feeling much more at ease now, knowing he was uncomfortable as well.

"So what do you normally get up to after work?" he asked.

"Well, I usually work late. Either I stay at the office or I take work home. Sometimes I go out with my girlfriends. Not girlfriends-girlfriends; friends who are girls." Zandi was embarrassed again, but she managed to laugh at what she'd said along with Rhulani.

"I'm pleased to hear that."

"And what do you get up to?"

"I like playing sports. I play soccer once a week, as well as tennis. The other times I go out with my boyfriends. Not boyfriends-boyfriends; friends who are boys."

They both laughed again.

"My brother, Sizwe, is mad about tennis."

"Maybe I can challenge him to a match sometime."

Zandi liked Rhulani's smile. It was warm and beautiful and seductive. She could smile with him even if she had no idea what he was smiling about.

The curried chicken was just as she had imagined it would be and she could see Rhulani was enjoying his seafood curry. Zandi wasn't a seafood person, but watching him eat prawns with his hands made her ask herself what it was that had made her decide she didn't like seafood.

In the end Rhulani must have noticed the way she was looking at him licking his lips, because he offered to share his food with her, after which she did the same with hers.

They ate and laughed, drank and laughed, talked and laughed. Rhulani had a good sense of humour and Zandi enjoyed every moment with him. They talked about blind dates, their love for Ringo's music, movies, books and family.

"Do you have any children?" Rhulani asked while they were on the topic of family.

"Yes, I have a seventeen-year-old boy," Zandi said and marvelled at how Rhulani almost choked on his drink. While he coughed, she continued, "I'm looking after him. He's my younger brother. I have no children of my own."

Now it was Rhulani's turn to look embarrassed and Zandi loved it. She thought he looked kind of cute when he was awkward, half closing his almond-shaped eyes. He also did something with his lower lip that made Zandi think she should keep on saying things that embarrassed him.

"Do you have children?" she asked.

"None that I know of," he said, watching Zandi's face closely. She hadn't expected an answer like that and shocked herself by also almost choking on her drink.

"Got you, didn't I? I have no kids, although I would really love to have some one day. Do you ever think about children?" Rhulani smiled at Zandi while she recovered her composure.

"My friend Neo is a nursery school teacher, so yes, I do sometimes think about kids. But never really about having my own . . . Do you have any siblings?" Zandi wondered if they were as good-looking as he was.

"Yes, I have a few siblings. In fact, many."

"How many is many?"

Rhulani played with his glass before answering. "I'll tell you some other day. We're currently undergoing an audit to determine exactly how many we are."

Zandi laughed. "You're a funny guy!"

"I get that all the time . . . I don't want to be inconsiderate, seeing that tomorrow is a workday. Shall I take you home?" he asked, looking at his watch.

Zandi peeped at her watch, which confirmed that it was probably a good idea to go.

On the way home she couldn't believe that a few hours earlier she had sat in the same car, afraid of being kidnapped; now all she wished for was to spend a little more time with Rhulani. He was funny, smart and sensitive, and he had warm hands.

As if he could read her mind, Rhulani took Zandi's hand in his and squeezed it, sending his warmth throughout her body all the way to her toes. At that moment she knew she liked him, not just as a friend that she could invite to Neo's wedding, but as someone who could potentially be more than just a friend to her.

When Rhulani pulled up the car in front of her flat, Zandi didn't want to go back to her boring flat. She wanted to stay out here with this man and laugh about all the funny things he had to say.

"I'll walk you to the door," he offered as they got out of the car.

They walked hand in hand to Zandi's door, where they stood as she got her keys out of her handbag.

"I enjoyed dinner but I enjoyed your company more," Rhulani said, brushing her cheek with the back of his hand.

"I enjoyed your company too. I had a wonderful time." Zandi's heart was racing from the touch of Rhulani's hand. She thought it was because the warmth of his hand was in sharp contrast to the cold air that had been brushing her cheeks since they got out of the car.

At that moment he moved closer to her. Zandi felt his warm body press against hers and the heat move rapidly from his body to hers. She felt momentarily as if she was about to go into a struggle for breath from the intensity of what she was feeling, and he seemed to know that, because his lips were on hers as if they were her only hope of survival.

She knew she couldn't stop him, even if she wanted to;

this was her kiss of life and she could feel her body coming to life. Her heart increased the rate at which it pumped blood to every cell of her body, which in turn demanded an increased supply of oxygen. Her lungs obliged by taking in more air and she felt the pace of her breathing quickening. She was alive and it felt so good!

Finally he let go, but she knew it was okay because now she would be able to continue breathing on her own. She couldn't stop smiling at this guy who had brought her back to life, and he happily smiled back.

"Oops, my keys," Zandi said, noticing that she didn't have them any more.

Rhulani picked up the keys, which had fallen to the ground, and handed them to her. He gave her a kiss on the cheek, bade her good night and walked down the stairs to his car. Zandi wished she could call after him and ask him to stay with her.

If only he didn't have to go.

4

Zandi rushed as she got ready for work. She couldn't believe it; she had overslept for the first time in what felt like forever. She knew it wasn't because of going to bed late; she was used to that. But she hadn't slept this well for ages.

Sizwe obviously didn't appreciate that; he was concerned about school. "You know I don't like being late," he mumbled as they finally got into the car.

"Have I ever dropped you late?" Zandi said, a little annoyed. "We're always there way before school starts. And today you're not going to be late either; you'll be just on time."

"You don't know that."

"Well, let's do some maths. Your school starts at eight; it's now twenty to, which means we still have twenty minutes to get you there. It takes us fifteen minutes to get to school, which gives you five minutes to walk to class. Even if you walk like a seventy-year-old man, you'll still be in class on time. On the other hand, if you walk like a seventeen-year-old boy, it will take only three minutes to get to class and you'll still have two minutes to do whatever you want." Zandi was now amused.

"Two minutes isn't enough to finish my homework."

"Sizwe Zungu, since when do you do that in the morning, in class?"

"It was a joke!" he grinned. Zandi couldn't help laughing at herself. She had been quite worked up by the thought of Sizwe neglecting his schoolwork, especially because she had been out having dinner with Rhulani instead of making sure that her brother's homework was done.

Zandi dropped Sizwe off and headed to Sandton to see a client.

When she arrived at work after her two-hour meeting, she was greeted by countless messages from Tondani. Zandi wasn't surprised at all; in fact, she was surprised that her friend wasn't there in person to interrogate her about the date with Rhulani. To amuse herself, Zandi decided not to return Tondani's calls, wanting to see how long it would be before she called again. Hardly ten minutes after she'd entered her office her phone rang.

Tondani was obviously desperate to hear how the date had gone. "Wow, just how late for work were you this morning? If I got a rand each time I left a message with your secretary, I'd be handing in my resignation right now."

"I wasn't late; I had an early-morning meeting."

"Don't lie. I bet you had a man sleep over at your house. You think I don't know how to read the signs?"

"What signs are you talking about?"

"Being late for work; you never arrive this late. Then you blame it on a meeting that your secretary knew nothing about. And then being defensive as soon as I started talking to you. Those are all telltale signs." Tondani had clearly already come to her own conclusions.

"I really did have a meeting, and my secretary knows

not to tell you where I am since the last time you gate-crashed my meeting, and I'm not being defensive because I really have no reason to be."

"Stop that, girlfriend. I don't appreciate you bringing up things from the past. So how did the date go last night?"

"Where do I begin? He's a wonderful man! He's warm, good-looking, funny . . . I'm so hooked. I feel like I owe you the world right now."

"You better remember you said that. So what did you get up to?"

"He picked me up at the flat, we went to the restaurant, we ate and he took me home again . . . We had a really good time."

"And? Surely that's not all?"

"We shared the most mind-blowing kiss. It was magical!"

"I'm so happy to hear that; it's time you got your groove back! But I guess you didn't even invite him in," Tondani probed.

"No, I did not. I wanted to, but I'd just met the man and I hadn't even done a background check on him. I didn't want to risk putting Sizwe's life and my own in danger." Zandi didn't believe that Rhulani would ever do anything to hurt her or her brother. She just needed to say something to distract Tondani. She didn't feel like sharing too much information about her date or their kiss.

"Stop thinking that everyone is a psycho! You're starting to sound like one yourself, being so suspicious of every-one."

"A girl just needs to be sure, that's all."

"Rhulani is Lutendo's friend. It's not like I just got him off the streets; there is nothing suspicious about the guy."

"I don't know."

"If it'll make you happy, I'll do the background check. So when are you seeing him again?"

"We're having dinner on Friday, and we're going for a picnic with Sizwe on Saturday." Zandi was already feeling as if she couldn't wait another day to see Rhulani again.

"He's meeting your family? Already? This sounds serious!"

Zandi was surprised by her friend's comment; she had certainly not seen things that way. Surely an invite for a picnic wasn't the same as a person wanting to meet the family?

"Tondani, there's nothing serious about eating sandwiches."

"Maybe to you, but for all you know it may be a big deal to him."

Zandi's heart skipped a beat at this realisation. Rhulani had not just invited her, he had asked her to bring her brother along. She really enjoyed Rhulani's company a lot, but she decided it was not a good idea to read too much into why he had invited Sizwe as well.

"You know, only time will tell if Rhulani is serious about me. I don't want to draw my own conclusions and have false hopes."

"Suit yourself, but I know the signs."

Zandi wasn't about to get into that with Tondani again, so she said her goodbyes and put the phone down.

For the rest of the day Rhulani dominated her thoughts. His smile, the warmth of his touch, his sense of humour. Zandi was a little surprised by the feelings this man stirred in her. She had just met him, but she was already missing him when he wasn't with her. She would think about something he'd said and smile to herself. She kept thinking about him feasting on the prawns and how he'd made eating with one's hands look so sexy. She just couldn't forget how romantic it had been to share food with him.

At the end of the day, concerned that she was spending too much time dreaming about Rhulani, Zandi told herself that he was just one of those people whom everyone tended to like. There was nothing wrong with her; anyone would miss Rhulani's company after spending time with him. She definitely was not falling for him.

On Friday Zandi opted for a cream shift dress that ended just above the knee. Her black high heels made her legs look almost endless, something she was very aware of and hoped would knock a few men off their feet. Hopefully her date as well. She pinned her braids loosely at the back to show off her pretty silver-and-black teardrop earrings.

When Rhulani arrived to pick her up, Zandi was glad that she had made the effort to look her best, otherwise she would have been embarrassed to be seen with him. He was looking dashing in a multicoloured striped shirt, black pants and a silver-grey jacket.

Zandi had chosen a cosy bistro in Illovo for dinner. Apart from the company, she enjoyed the soft music, the magical lighting, her crunchy walnut salad with succulent roast beef, and watching Rhulani savour every mouthful of his fillet with grilled vegetables.

After their meal Rhulani suggested that they share crème brûlée for dessert. Although Zandi would have been happy to have the dessert all to herself, she found that sharing with him made it so much more enjoyable. The crème brûlée was sweet, but Zandi found the kiss she shared with Rhulani at the end of the evening sweeter than anything she had ever tasted.

Saturday was the perfect day for a picnic. The weather was warm, with a cool breeze that made being outdoors a pleasant experience. Zandi was looking forward to spending time surrounded by green trees that were actually alive and breathing some clean, fresh air. She wished Sizwe would also show some excitement.

"Do we really need to go?" her brother asked for the third time as he helped her pack the basket.

"It's good to go out sometimes and unwind a bit. What do you do on weekends anyway? Study, play computer games, sit around . . . Don't you miss the green countryside of Nongoma?"

Zandi often longed for home. She missed the bright red soil and the dusty roads, the pathways that people and livestock had forged, winding from one house to the other. She missed the hills and the valleys and all the greenery. She missed seeing cattle and goats grazing in the fields without a care in the world, and the sound of the birds that never got tired of singing all day. But it seemed Sizwe didn't like to talk about Nongoma.

"This Rhulani, is he your boyfriend?"

"No, he's just a friend. And guess what, he's a tennis player. Maybe you can play together sometime; it will be good practice for you," Zandi said, trying to change the subject. True, Rhulani wasn't her boyfriend, but why had her brother's question made her tingle all over?

Sizwe just shrugged his shoulders and said, "We'll see."

By the time Rhulani arrived, Zandi was no longer sure whether a picnic with him and Sizwe was such a good idea after all. She was looking forward to it, but her brother wasn't very keen. On the other hand, she didn't see any harm in him spending a Saturday afternoon with someone whom he could discuss sports with for a change. She had tried all she could to understand soccer, even looking up the term "offside" in a dictionary, but the truth was she still didn't get it.

Sizwe placed the basket his sister had packed with plates and cutlery in the boot of the car, next to the one with food Rhulani had brought.

As Zandi got into the seat beside him, Rhulani looked at her red floral summer dress and started to say "Lovely dress" but quickly changed it to "Lovely day" when he saw her brother getting into the back seat. Zandi couldn't contain her grin at Rhulani's embarrassment as he smiled somewhat sheepishly at her.

"So you're the much-talked-about Sizwe?" Rhulani asked after greetings had been exchanged.

"I am Sizwe. Much talked about? Not here, maybe in Nongoma, but not here."

Zandi saw that her brother was trying his best not to be disrespectful, but he would obviously much rather have been somewhere else.

If Rhulani picked it up, he decided not to take it too seriously. "I certainly didn't hear about you from Nongoma, so there are people who talk about you here too. What about the guys you go to school with?"

"I don't think so. I'm not friends with anyone."

Rhulani acted surprised. "You don't have friends at school?"

"Well . . . I only came to Joburg this year, so I don't know many people, and most of them don't know me either."

Zandi couldn't believe her ears. "You told me you'd made friends."

Sizwe just looked out of the window and said nothing.

"But I've been told you play tennis. Sport should help you make friends. Get involved in tournaments, then people will start to know you. Do you ever take part in tournaments?"

Sizwe shook his head. Rhulani decided to change the course of the conversation when they pulled into the Johannesburg botanical gardens in Emmarentia. "What school do you go to?"

"Fourways High."

"Serious? I was there like fifty years ago. But then I was very naughty and got into all kinds of trouble and was expelled. It's a great school; I realised that a few years later

43

when I was more mature, and tried to get back in there again. Unfortunately the teachers remembered the trouble I used to cause and didn't want me anywhere near their school again." Rhulani tried to look as sad as possible as Zandi and Sizwe laughed at his story.

They found a nice spot for the picnic under a large tree and started unpacking their baskets onto a blanket. Rhulani had brought beef wraps, Greek salad, chicken strips with a jalapeño dip, fruit salad and red grape juice.

"I told my brother you could challenge each other to a game of tennis sometime," Zandi said as she poured everyone some juice.

"Yes, you mentioned that he was a worthy opponent. What do you say, Sizwe?"

"I don't know; I haven't played for a long time. I'm just an amateur," Sizwe answered with no excitement in his voice.

"Well then, we'll just have to fast-track you into being a pro!"

Sizwe laughed despite himself and looked at Rhulani with something like surprise.

Soon Zandi could see a distinct change in her brother's manner. Before they left the house he would have paid her to leave him behind; now it was as if he couldn't smile enough. He seemed to be enjoying Rhulani's company as much as she was.

After they had eaten and rested in the shade, Rhulani and Sizwe decided to go for a walk, but Zandi chose to stay in the shade and enjoy the cool breeze.

She was starting to drift into sleep when she felt a hand on her face brushing her braids aside, and woke with a start.

"Where's Sizwe?" Zandi asked in a panic when she looked up and saw Rhulani was alone.

"We met some boys his age and they invited him to play soccer with them. I thought I'd leave him to make friends, so I came back to have some time alone with you." Rhulani lay down on the blanket beside Zandi as she started to relax again. Reaching for a chicken strip, he dipped it in the sauce and offered her a bite.

"Oops! I must sit up first. I'm getting the dip all over my face," Zandi said, trying to sit up, but Rhulani stopped her with his other hand.

"Please don't. That's the whole point."

5

The first thing that came to Zandi's mind when she woke up on Monday morning was that she was sure she was in love. This was what it was supposed to feel like; this was what it had felt like with Jeffrey.

She had met him on campus while having lunch with friends. Jeffrey knew some of the girls she was sitting with and asked if he could join them since there were no free tables. Zandi liked him from the moment they were introduced, and felt annoyed that she and Jeffrey couldn't have a private conversation with all the girls there. To make matters worse, she had to rush off to a test shortly afterwards.

For weeks after their brief meeting, Zandi walked around campus wishing to see him, but she had no idea how to trace a guy she knew only as Jeffrey. She couldn't get herself to ask the girls who knew him, because she didn't want to be seen as someone who chased after guys.

But then on the last day of class she found herself sitting next to Jeffrey, who admitted he had attended no lectures the whole term until that day. For her that was a sign that they were meant to be together. For Jeffrey it was a relief to find someone who could lend him notes and help him prepare for the exam, which was only two weeks away.

They grew close in a very short space of time and started dating. Zandi had always looked forward to the day when she would marry the man that fate had brought to her, but it later turned out that he had other plans.

Now, five years since she'd met Jeffrey, she was experiencing that feeling all over again. Rhulani had touched her heart in a special kind of way. It was for that reason that Zandi was quick to shake off the feeling of guilt because she had not even touched her laptop since leaving the office for the weekend.

Dinner on Friday was an experience she was still struggling to articulate; maybe she even needed to come up with some new words that were not in the dictionary. The picnic on Saturday had made her understand why some people pack their lunch and go and eat it outside on the grass, leaving the luxury of their comfortable homes. And she'd always thought of chicken strips as boring, but at their picnic Rhulani had made her see them in a totally different light.

But most importantly, she was glad that he and Sizwe were getting along so well. They had ended on a good note on Saturday after the picnic, and Rhulani had fetched her brother for a tennis game on Sunday afternoon. From what Zandi had heard, the game ended up being more of a coaching session, and Sizwe couldn't stop singing Rhulani's praises. She thought it was a good thing, because Rhulani was convinced that taking part in sports would help the boy make friends at school.

Zandi sat in her office, staring at her phone and wondering if she should give Rhulani a call. She had called him before her morning meeting to thank him for the picnic and for spending time with Sizwe, although she had been disappointed to find that he had just woken up. She didn't want to seem too clingy. Surely calling a guy you have just met more than twice a day is not allowed?

On the other hand, why not call if she was thinking of doing that the whole time? Why not just pick up the phone? Then at least her thoughts would be put to rest. She honestly felt breaking the rules was okay, given that she liked hearing Rhulani's voice so much. Zandi dialled his number.

When he answered the phone he sounded a little uncertain. "Zandi?"

"Hi, Rhulani, did I get you at a bad time?" She was already feeling silly for deciding to call him, remembering that people were usually busy during the day.

"I'm on my way to a meeting. What did you want to say?"

"I just wanted to say hi, that's all." Zandi tried to swallow her embarrassment. Just wanted to say hi! How many times did she need to greet the same person in one day?

"But we already spoke this morning."

"Yes, you're right, we did. But I was rushing off to a meeting and you'd just woken up . . ."

"Well, now *I'm* rushing to get to a meeting."

Zandi just wanted to hang up and put an end to her embarrassment. Maybe even destroy her phone to avoid embarrassing herself again in future.

"Of course. We'll speak later then!"

Rhulani put down the phone and Zandi was left stunned. She had no idea what had just happened. She'd imagined that he would be happy to hear her voice again, but obviously she had been mistaken. Perhaps Rhulani was rushing off to a very important meeting which he was nervous about, she hoped and crossed her fingers.

On Wednesday Zandi drove to a restaurant for dinner with Rhulani. She had told him not to pick her up as she would be coming from work. On arrival, she promised herself that she would not bring up what had happened on the phone on Monday; she didn't want to spoil the evening. As soon as she saw him sitting there, waiting for her, she felt a kind of relief. It had been a long day at work and she was tired. Seeing Rhulani seemed to relax all the muscles that were tense in her body, and so did the warm red tones that were used throughout the restaurant on the walls and in the lighting.

When she arrived at the table, he got up and pulled a chair out for her. Zandi appreciated this gentlemanly gesture. She also appreciated how handsome he looked in a white shirt and formal black trousers.

"I thought you weren't going to show up," Rhulani said flatly once she was seated. Zandi was slightly late and she wondered if his statement was meant to make her feel bad about it.

"But here I am. I like to surprise people," she said with a smile, having decided to brush off his comment.

"I don't like to be surprised."

49

Zandi thought Rhulani sounded cold and decided that he was not in a good mood. She was feeling a bit lost, not knowing what topics would be okay to talk about to a moody man she didn't know much about. Work seemed like a safe option.

"I realise I haven't even asked you what you do for a living. You do work, don't you?"

At least Rhulani got the humour in Zandi's question and grinned.

"Yes, I do work. I'm a business strategist," he said. She was relieved to see the smile back on his handsome face.

"I'd be lying if I said I knew any business strategists. What exactly do you do?"

Rhulani was quiet for a bit, as if trying to put his thoughts together before he answered.

"My work is quite complex. I run my own consultancy. I help businesses with their strategies. Some companies are already deep in trouble; others just want to avoid getting into it in future."

"Sounds like a lot of long hours."

"It's tough, but as a rule I don't work later than six. I think it's important to have a healthy balance between your career and private life."

Zandi wondered if Rhulani was trying to say something about her work habits.

"Well, it sounds like your kind of job is fun."

"If you knew how much work was involved, you wouldn't say that. It's not just a matter of going to the company that has a crisis and telling everyone to do ABC and the next day everything goes back to normal. You need to do a lot of background research and find out what decisions they had made in the past that led to them being in the situation they are in, and people aren't always willing to admit to their mistakes."

Zandi was starting to feel uncomfortable. Bad day or not, she didn't understand why Rhulani was speaking to her as if she was nowhere near his level and understood nothing about how companies operated. True, she didn't know exactly what business strategists did, but she was a smart woman and didn't appreciate him making it sound as if she had the intelligence of a six-year-old.

"Surely as a specialist you have ways of getting around those issues?" Zandi was doing her best to keep her cool.

"That's correct, but at the end of the day the work drains you. It's really tough." It seemed Rhulani was bent on stressing just how complicated and hard his kind of work was. Zandi didn't like people who made it sound as if what they did was superior. Each person contributed to the economy in his or her own way.

"Oh, well, work is hard, whichever way you look at it," she said firmly.

"I disagree. Some people have it easy. For instance, I went to the bank today and I lost count of how many queues I had to stand in before I got some excuse for service. Somewhere someone was obviously not doing their job." Rhulani sounded very sure of what he was saying. Then he added, "I hope you don't work at a bank."

Zandi wondered if she really wanted to hear the business strategist's view on economists and whether they did their job properly. "I'm an economist and I work for a company called Modise & Associates."

Rhulani frowned. "Never heard of such a company before. I've worked with most of the big players in the finance sector."

He was busy chewing his steak. Zandi thought it had to taste really bad for him to be making such comments, or maybe he was just finding it difficult to chew. If that was the case, he should have also ordered the soft-textured baked fish she was having.

"I prefer working in a smaller company, and since I started working there, Modise & Associates has really grown. I'm sure you'll start hearing about us soon."

"I suppose being an economist means you work a lot of long hours?"

"Most of the time, depending on deadlines. Actually, I constantly feel like my job is driven by deadlines."

"So you spend most of your time at the office?"

Zandi wondered why this was suddenly feeling like an interrogation, maybe to determine what decisions she had made in the past that led her to be in the situation she was in right now.

"Yes. Although not so much since Sizwe came to stay with me. But I still do a lot of work at home in the evenings."

"Not good when you're a wife and mother," Rhulani said scornfully.

Zandi realised it had been a mistake to think that talking about work was a safe option. She had no idea she would find herself under so much attack for reasons she could not figure out.

"The last time I checked I had neither a husband nor children, so I don't have to feel guilty that I spend so much of my time working. What's more, I find my job very rewarding." Zandi was getting frustrated; there was absolutely no need for her to justify herself to Rhulani and yet she was unwillingly doing just that.

"I suppose you don't feel guilty about leaving your mother alone in Nongoma either?"

"She's an independent woman who is very capable of looking after herself, and she understands that I need to work." Who did this man think he was and what did it matter to him what she chose to do with her time and family?

"I'm sure your mother understands, but you don't need to be away from home to be able to work." Apparently Rhulani was not about to let this one go so easily.

"I couldn't have the kind of job I have right now if I was living in Nongoma. Unfortunately a person sometimes needs to make sacrifices. I'm sure you've had to make sacrifices at some stage in your life." She didn't care any more if she hurt his feelings or if she made him hate her. At least then they'd be even.

Rhulani just raised his shoulders and let them drop again. Zandi didn't feel like arguing, but she definitely felt a sudden dislike for him. He obviously saw himself as an important guy who kept the world running smoothly, and didn't think much of her and everyone at Modise & Associates. She was also shocked by his rudeness. She decided he was just plain bad-mannered, or else he had decided he wasn't interested in her and was being mean to get rid of her. Either way, Zandi didn't have any intention of seeing him again.

But not wanting to fall into the same category of impolite people as Rhulani, she resolved not to walk out on their dinner date just because she was upset. They finished their meal and Zandi had some ice cream, much to Rhulani's disapproval, because he didn't like ice cream. She didn't care; as long as she was putting up with his stories about his job and the strategies he had come up with to save different companies that were in trouble, he simply had to put up with her enjoying her ice cream.

Eventually Zandi felt she had heard enough strategies to start her own consultation business and she was determined to change the topic. "So where do you know Lutendo from? I hear you're good friends."

"Yes, we are; he is also one of my clients. Do you know how much trouble that engineering consultancy of theirs was in?"

Zandi could have yawned, but she insisted on being polite. Her efforts to change the topic had taken her right back to where she was before. "No, I had no idea!"

"Yes, deep trouble. Most people don't realise how difficult it is to run a company. Writing a business plan is the easy part. They had huge financial and operational problems; that's why Lutendo is so very grateful to me." Rhulani clearly thought of himself as the most important person in the world. Everybody else created problems, which he then solved.

"I suppose it's good to have someone like you around," Zandi said as they got up to leave, grateful that she didn't have to put up with him much longer.

"Where are you parked?" Rhulani asked when they got to the car park.

"Oh, you don't need to walk me there. Thanks for dinner." Zandi figured the sooner she parted ways with Rhulani, the better.

"I'm not letting you walk to your car alone. What kind of a man would I be?"

Zandi could think of a few appropriate answers, but she appreciated the gesture and smiled slightly. They walked to her car in silence while she wondered whether Rhulani was doing this because he expected a kiss. If that was the case, he was going to be very disappointed.

They got to her car and Rhulani opened the door. "I really enjoyed dinner with you tonight."

"I'm glad you did." Zandi was not going to say she had enjoyed the evening, because she hadn't. The food had been enjoyable, but not the company. She stood next to Rhulani, searching his face to understand why he had behaved the way he did tonight, but she couldn't find an explanation. Just a week ago she had enjoyed being with him so much that she didn't want him to go, but now she couldn't wait to go home.

"Maybe you can come over to my place for lunch or dinner on Saturday?"

Zandi didn't think there was a chance of that ever happening. "I'll have to get back to you on that one. Thanks for the evening. Good night."

As she was getting into her car, Zandi felt her body brush against Rhulani, who was standing a little too close to the door. It was slight, it was brief, but it was unmistakable. She held her breath as the current went through her body, leaving no cell untouched. Then she took a deep breath and settled into her seat.

"So I might see you on Saturday?" asked the seductive voice.

Zandi had to focus hard on why she couldn't let the voice get to her. "Yes, Saturday, maybe."

She reached for the door that Rhulani still held open. She was about to close it when he handed her something.

"What's this?"

"My business card. You might want to tell your boss to give me a ring," Rhulani said, and walked away.

Zandi slammed the door of her car, hard.

6

The last thing Zandi did before getting into bed was to leave a message on Tondani's phone to say she couldn't believe she had made her go out with such a rude man. Apparently his strategy was to soften you up before he struck, making the strike all the more painful. She couldn't believe she had wasted an entire evening talking to a man who enjoyed criticising her for no reason at all and rambling on about how wonderful he was, and how everybody else was not nearly good enough. Zandi had decided she didn't want anything to do with Rhulani any more and her friend had to see to it that he got the message.

The following morning Zandi received a call from Tondani.

"Girlfriend, why are you leaving messages on my phone in a foreign language?"

"What?" Zandi was confused. She had been upset, but the message she'd left was definitely not in a strange language.

"What I'm saying is, I don't understand what's your problem with Rhulani. I thought you couldn't take a breath without thinking about the guy."

"That was before yesterday. He was so rude, and for absolutely no reason."

"Are you sure?"

"Am I sure he was rude? Do you know what torture I went through last night? Are you my friend or his?" Zandi was starting to get upset about Tondani's remarks.

"Of course I'm your friend! I just don't understand; the first date is supposed to be the worst and you seemed to have come out of that pretty well. What went wrong? Did you tell him you suspected him of being a psycho? Because if you did, he's not going to stick around."

"You know, I should've told him just that, because he definitely does have psycho tendencies. Our first date went great; he was very considerate and charming. Our second date was also great; the picnic was awesome. But yesterday he was a total monster!" Zandi felt anger building up inside her. What had happened to make the Rhulani she'd liked so much in the past week someone she now despised? She wanted the good guy back.

Tondani sighed. "Maybe you need to take it easy; you haven't been on a date for years. Don't beat yourself up about the one dinner that went wrong."

"I'm not beating myself up about it. I should beat *you* up for putting me in that situation. The guy thinks he's the best thing since colour-stay lip gloss. I mean, really now," Zandi said, rolling her eyes.

"Can you blame him? He was just feeling insecure. You're smart, beautiful, successful . . . any man would feel like he has to prove that he can do cartwheels backwards before he gets the nod."

"I felt like he was trying to prove that I don't deserve a

man who can do cartwheels backwards. He practically told me I was a wannabe."

"Girl, just give the guy a break."

After Zandi had put the phone down, she wondered whether Rhulani truly deserved to be given a chance. He had acted in a gentlemanly fashion towards her on all their dates. Her brother liked him and he clearly liked the boy enough to spend part of his weekend playing tennis with him. Zandi appreciated his help because Sizwe seemed much happier lately, and certainly more confident. But then there was last night.

The more she thought about it, the more Zandi was convinced Rhulani was trying to get rid of her – for whatever reason. Maybe he had decided after the three dates that he didn't like her? Or that he didn't like Sizwe? Or that he liked neither her nor Sizwe? He hadn't been shy to voice issues he had with her family at the dinner last night. Or maybe he had an ex-girlfriend he'd reconciled with and couldn't get himself to tell her about it. Zandi simply couldn't figure it out.

But then again, everyone had off days.

After a while Zandi decided she would give Rhulani another chance. Maybe he'd had an extremely bad day that had made it impossible for him to be nice.

Zandi did her best to get the bad dinner experience out of her mind. She had expected an explanation or apology, but when she got neither, she decided not to judge Rhulani. She had no idea what was going on with him on Wednesday, and she realised it wasn't fair to label him as rude based on just that one night.

For that reason Zandi decided to take Tondani's advice and informed Rhulani that she would have lunch with him. After she had reconsidered, she actually thought it was romantic of him to ask her to come to his place. She thought it was about time too. Before she met Jeffrey, her ideal man was definitely someone who would enjoy cooking for her. But Jeffrey wasn't much of a cook. Although he sometimes did try, leaving her with a kitchen that needed a whole army to clean it, at best, or food poisoning, at worst. Eventually she had got over her fantasy of a man who brings her breakfast in bed.

This time she was hopeful. Besides having been obviously angry about something on their last date, Rhulani seemed every bit like the kind of man who would enjoy spoiling a lady. She had picked that up from the little things he did: the way he got up and pulled out a chair for her at a restaurant, or walked her to her car, or called to find out if she had arrived home safely. She knew she couldn't take any of these gestures to mean much, since it was still early days, but she couldn't recall Jeffrey doing any of those things, even in the early days. Because of this she was hopeful that Rhulani would finally bring her fantasies of a man who loves cooking for her to life, especially since he had willingly offered to cook lunch without bribes of a massage or anything of the kind.

Having resolved to drive herself to his place in Midrand, Zandi hoped she wouldn't get lost. She had thought it wouldn't be a good idea for Rhulani to come and fetch her all the way from Fourways, because then he would need to cook beforehand and the food would get cold. Or it would mean he could only cook after fetching her, which was not what she had in mind.

She wanted to arrive at his place and be welcomed by the aroma of food cooking on the stove and know that he went to all the trouble and slaved over the stove just for her. As she smiled at the thought, it was easier for her to put all that was said at their last date behind her. The true Rhulani was the gentleman she had got to know during their first three dates, and that was the only impression of him she wanted to keep with her.

Zandi kept her eyes fixed on the road, not wanting to miss a turn-off and risk being late for the lunch she had dreamt about all her adult life. She was quite relieved when she turned into the road that was meant to take her straight to Rhulani's place, and even more relieved when she saw the gate right in front of her. As she drove through and found parking, she started wondering whether Rhulani would be busy setting the table by now. If not, she would be happy to help with that part.

She walked up to the second floor and knocked softly, not wanting to sound desperate. After a few more knocks with no answer, she rapped a bit louder, but there was still no answer. Zandi couldn't help but panic. Had Rhulani forgotten that she was coming for lunch? Wasn't he in there cooking for her? She reached for her cellphone, not sure if she could ever forgive him if he wasn't home at that moment.

The voice that answered the phone didn't do much to put Zandi's mind at ease. She thought Rhulani sounded rather surprised, which made her a little upset.

"I'm at the door."

"I'll be there now."

She was relieved that at least he was home.

When Rhulani finally opened the door, Zandi was welcomed into a very spacious modern lounge. A large black leather couch stood on one side of the room and a smaller cream leather couch was on the side adjacent to it. The wooden coffee table was black and it had been placed on a grey rug. There was a large mirror mounted on the wall behind the black couch and against the wall opposite it was a TV.

Zandi immediately liked the simple elegance of the place, and then thought to herself again that it wasn't for her to like. She turned her attention from the furnishings to Rhulani, who looked casual in a grey golf shirt and dark-blue clam diggers. Zandi thought he looked even more handsome in casual wear and was pleased that she had agreed to lunch. She could freely ogle his arms since he wasn't wearing a long-sleeved shirt today.

"So my directions weren't too bad?" Rhulani asked as he offered her a seat.

"They were quite good, actually; I didn't need to stop once to ask the way. Were you sleeping?" Zandi couldn't help noticing that he looked like someone who had just woken up. And she couldn't help noticing that there was no sign at all that he had been busy cooking before she arrived. And unless she had suddenly lost her sense of smell, there was not even the slightest aroma of food cooking.

Rhulani smiled and then yawned as he went ahead and stretched himself. "I don't know what happened to me. I just fell asleep on the couch. The phone woke me; I must have slept for about two hours. I'm so tired today, but I don't know why."

Zandi was now definitely sure that there was no lunch cooking in the kitchen. She was disappointed at the thought of having to wait while Rhulani cooked, as she was already feeling starved.

"You probably just needed some rest."

He brushed the top of his head with his hand. "I guess so. And maybe I didn't think you'd make it for lunch."

"Why would you think that? I called earlier to confirm."

"Oh well, there's always work that can come up."

Zandi realised where Rhulani's comments were going. She didn't want a repeat of Wednesday night, so she decided to step away from the subject of work before it got out of hand. "My weekends are more flexible."

"If you're like me, you must be starving," Rhulani said as he got up and put some music on.

Zandi was relieved that the thoughtful man was back. "Yes, I am. I haven't eaten anything since breakfast."

Rhulani was standing in the middle of the lounge with his hands on his hips. She wondered whether he had any idea how she felt, seeing him look like that, showing off his strong arms.

"And I haven't eaten a home-cooked meal in a while,

63

being the bachelor that I am," he said in his sexy voice. "I had better show you the kitchen."

"Excuse me?" Zandi had been lost in thought and wondered if she'd misunderstood him.

"So that you can make us lunch. You *can* cook, right?"

Zandi was so shocked that she wondered if she would even manage to get up from where she was sitting.

7

Zandi was confused. She had never met a man who'd been as rude to her as Rhulani, especially since she thought he was supposed to be doing his best to impress her. Unless a very bad friend of his was giving him the wrong kind of advice on how to impress a lady, she thought, Rhulani was a sexist male who obviously didn't think much of women. He had made it sound as if her job was not important. Then he scoffed at her decision to leave home because of her career, and yesterday he chuckled at her suggestion that he make lunch for them. She didn't think men like him still existed, but she was obviously wrong.

But the very same Rhulani would turn around and act all gentlemanly, opening the door for her or walking her to her car. Why was he giving her these mixed signals? Was he maybe playing hard to get? She remembered when she was in her early twenties it was the girls who played hard to get, but maybe things had changed during the past ten years? How else could she explain the fact that the man she had shared a passionate kiss with just a week ago had suddenly turned into someone she couldn't even imagine kissing any more?

The more Zandi played through the events of the past week in her mind, the more difficult it was for her to shake the feeling that maybe Rhulani had an ex-girlfriend whom he'd now made up with. Surely that would explain his strange behaviour? As much as she hated snooping, Zandi hadn't been able to stop herself from looking around in his flat for signs of a girl spending too much time there.

She had looked in the bathroom and briefly glanced into Rhulani's room to see if she could find anything girly or pink. She found neither, but the place was spotlessly clean, so she couldn't really discount the possibility that he might have removed any traces of the girl.

Zandi just started to stress even more. The last thing she wanted was to be the other woman; she had heard too many scary stories ever to put herself in that situation. She loved her face the way it was without having it scratched by an angry girlfriend. There were moments when she felt like being upfront and asking Rhulani if he had made up with his ex-girlfriend and was now trying to get rid of her, but just then he would look at her with eyes that told her he cared about her and she didn't have to worry about anything. The truth was that she cared about him too. That is, she did until she went to bed last night.

This morning she'd woken up and realised that Zandi Zungu was done with the man called Rhulani Mhinga. She'd had enough of his negative comments, and she had better things to do with her time than spend it with someone like him. His seductive smile and magical voice were not enough. Zandi needed a man who could find it in himself to support her, even if he didn't agree with the choices she'd made; a man who wouldn't criticise her so ruthlessly but rather give constructive advice where he felt she could improve. Would it really kill Rhulani to be that kind of man?

Zandi stared at her laptop and wondered why it didn't have answers to this most important question. She couldn't believe that after everything she had been through with Rhulani, she was back on her couch, working the night shift on a weekend and wearing ugly tracksuit pants.

Zandi answered her ringing phone and immediately wished she hadn't. She didn't want to discuss matters of the heart with Tondani any more. "I hope this isn't about Rhulani again."

"Who? No, not even close . . . I just wanted to ask if we could have the dinner at your place."

"What dinner?"

"Neo and Thabo's pre-wedding dinner. We were planning on having it at my place. But unfortunately my in-laws are here and they're in bed by seven, so I wouldn't want to keep them awake."

Zandi had completely forgotten about the dinner, which was only a few days away, on Wednesday evening. "My flat is so small. Can't you just invite your in-laws to join us?"

"Believe me, that wouldn't be a good idea. We can work some magic with your place. After all, we're talking ten people at most."

"What am I supposed to do with Sizwe?"

"It's only dinner, Zandi; just for an hour or two. He can join us."

Zandi took a few seconds to consider and then said,

"Invite a few single men, will you. I still need a date for the wedding."

"I thought you'd never ask. Sweet dreams!"

Zandi wasn't entirely sure about the single men or about the dinner being at her flat, but who was she to prevent life from continuing? She had to move on from Rhulani, if only to find herself a date for the wedding.

On the day of the dinner Zandi walked into her flat and almost didn't recognise her own living area. Tondani had decorated the whole place in creamy white drapings. The table was covered with a creamy white cloth and all the plates and dishes were creamy white. The chairs were covered with loose creamy white cloths. The romantic feel was enhanced by the many candles that were placed along the centre of the long table. Four standing lights stood at the corners of the room. The centrepiece was a large crystal bowl that was filled with what looked like artificial ice cubes with light shining from inside them. Zandi thought Tondani had done a good job with the décor, and her friend was still hard at work with the caterer setting out the platters.

Zandi greeted Tondani and realised for the first time that something was missing. "Where's my couch?"

"Oh, you know, I've always wanted to get rid of that thing, and there's always someone willing to take something for free. Maybe now you'll go out more and actually do something about getting a date and a boyfriend." Tondani winked and went back to organising spring rolls on a platter.

"Why did I ever give you my keys?! Why did I ever agree to this dinner being at my place?!"

"Stop stressing! I would never have guessed you had such a bond with that couch. It's on the balcony because I needed to make space in here. I brought my foldaway table and some chairs to lengthen your dinner table. Why don't you go get ready?"

Zandi took a deep breath. She was still trying to get used to the idea that in an hour's time there would be a handful of single men in her house. She wouldn't be so stressed if she only had to smile at them and make conversation, but on top of that she had to get one of them to agree to be her date for the wedding. She went to her room, wishing she could take a long, relaxing bath. But there was no time; she had to settle for a quick shower.

After that Zandi put on a long grey dress in flowing chiffon. She liked the way the strapless design showed off her beautiful shoulders and arms. It was a simple dress, but it made her look every inch a princess. To complete the look, she pinned her braids up into a bun. She was ready to get herself a date.

Before the guests started to arrive, Zandi studied the seating plan that Tondani had drawn up. She was impressed that she would be sitting between two men but surprised that the man on her one side was to be Tondani's brother. "Why is your brother coming here?"

"Oh, he's been dumped – again! He's been feeling down about the whole thing so I thought, why not invite him. He might just meet someone who'll be for keeps this time."

"Then why not seat him next to a single woman?"

"Sorry to point it out to you, girl, but in case you haven't noticed, you are a single woman. Maybe you should give him a chance; he's a sweetheart."

Zandi sighed but decided to leave it at that. She would just have to focus all her attention on the one whose name was Simphiwe. On second thoughts, she realised it would probably not have been such a good idea to try and juggle two guys at the same time, given her recent history with men.

The guests started arriving shortly before seven, and within fifteen minutes everyone was there except Tondani's brother, whom Zandi couldn't care less about. In fact, knowing how unreliable he was, she wasn't even expecting him to show up at all.

As if Tondani was thinking the same thoughts as her friend, she announced that the guests could sit down and start dinner so long; her brother would join them during the course of the meal.

"Hi, I'm Simphiwe," the man to Zandi's right greeted her after they had taken their seats.

"I'm Zandi, nice to meet you," she smiled back at him.

"Ah, the hostess. Nice place you have here," Simphiwe said, looking around them.

"Thank you. But Tondani made it look way nicer than it really is." And in her mind she added, "You look nice too." Simphiwe had a likeable face. He was most probably in his thirties but looked younger than that. Zandi thought his chubby cheeks were adorable when he smiled. His head was shaved clean and so was his face, except for a moustache.

Dinner was a mixed roast of beef, ostrich, chicken and sausage. The meat was served with roast vegetables and basmati rice. Just the aroma of the food was enough to rouse Zandi's appetite.

"This must be one of the best roasts I've ever tasted; the meat is so tender," she said after she had taken a bite of her food.

"Thank you."

Zandi was confused by Simphiwe's answer. "I meant the roast." This time she made sure to point at her plate with her fork.

Simphiwe looked at her, a little puzzled, which confused Zandi even more. Then he said, "Oh, uhm . . . it seems you don't know. I catered for the dinner."

"You?" she gasped. "You made the food?"

Simphiwe nodded.

"But when I came home there was a woman here who I thought was the caterer."

"That's my assistant. I had to go home and get ready to come back for the dinner."

Zandi wondered if this was her lucky day. Not only could Simphiwe cook, he was a chef as well! All she had to do now was get him to be her date for the wedding.

About ten minutes after everyone had taken their seats, the doorbell rang. Zandi shot a look at Tondani; she wasn't about to be disturbed just because her friend's brother couldn't be on time.

Tondani got up to open the door and Zandi was shocked to see Rhulani standing there. She saw him look at the only empty seat at the table, and then at her. She thought he looked as handsome as the first day she'd met him. The only difference was that now she couldn't tell if his presence still had an effect on her or not.

Rhulani made his way to the seat beside Zandi, and she raised an eyebrow at Tondani, who just smiled back.

"Hi there, Zandi," Rhulani greeted after he had made himself comfortable.

"Hi, Rhulani," she answered and immediately resumed her conversation with Simphiwe. She understood now. Tondani had invited Rhulani without telling her about it. Her friend had tactically seated him next to her at the table and used her brother as a cover so that Zandi would not find out until the last minute.

Zandi had no intention of making this easy for Tondani or Rhulani. She was going to focus all her attention on Simphiwe, as she had previously intended doing. But unfortunately she found ignoring Rhulani easier said than done. Even when she had her back to him, she was aware of him talking to the man opposite him, apparently not interested in the lady sitting on his other side.

At some stage Rhulani leaned towards her and whispered, "You're looking good tonight."

Zandi was taken by surprise. She had almost forgotten just how seductive his voice could be and what kind of emotions it was capable of stirring in her. She was taken back to three weeks previously, when all she wanted was to be with

Rhulani. But so much had happened since then. So much had been said that made Zandi see him differently. It didn't matter how the sound of his voice made her feel; she was now in control of her life and he was not the kind of man she needed around. She was not going to be distracted.

Rhulani's move had been very swift and Zandi didn't think anyone at the table had seen or heard him, so she decided to pretend that she hadn't either. She turned to him and asked, "Enjoying the food?"

"It's really good," Rhulani said and gave her a long, lingering look.

Zandi opened her mouth to say something but only managed a gasp. She was momentarily lost in Rhulani's eyes; those warm, dark, seductive eyes that looked like a calm ocean but stirred the space around her into a rough sea. She had not expected him to be at the dinner and she certainly hadn't braced herself to survive any storms. She forced herself to think about Simphiwe sitting on her other side; he could cook and he made the most tender roast.

"Would you believe that Simphiwe here made the food?" Zandi tried hard to regain her composure as she included the chef in their conversation. She had decided that conversing with Rhulani alone was stepping into dangerous territory.

"Hi, I'm Simphiwe." He extended his hand.

"Rhulani. Pleased to meet you."

"I was just saying to Rhulani that you make the best food I've ever tasted. Maybe you can tell us how you got to be such a great chef."

Simphiwe smiled broadly at her compliment, but Zandi was suddenly afraid that Rhulani was about to cut through his plate with the knife in his hand.

"My mother owned a small catering company. As a student I had to work for her to earn pocket money. There were two options: washing the dishes or helping her prepare food. I wasn't into dirty dishes, so I tried hard to learn to cook. Later on I trained as a chef and when my mother retired, I decided to take over the business."

At times Zandi looked at Rhulani's dark skin gleaming like chocolate. She got the feeling that if it could change colour, it would be slowly turning green with envy.

"So you never had any hang-ups about being a guy in an apron?"

"Why? As far as I know, ladies love a man wearing an apron."

Zandi thought Simphiwe had a point, but Rhulani was of a different view. He spoke with a mouth full of food. "Maybe some men just don't think they look good in an apron."

Zandi ignored the urge to reply that she doubted whether a man who spoke with his mouth full of food would look good in an apron. Instead, she excused herself and left the table.

She went to the kitchen and found Tondani busy taking the dessert out of the fridge.

"Why did you do that?"

"You mean take the dessert out of the fridge?"

"You know what I'm talking about. Why did you invite Rhulani?"

"So that the two of you would realise just how great you are for each other! I don't know what you're both afraid of."

"You know what, this is Neo and Thabo's evening. Let's not talk about Rhulani and me."

When Zandi turned around, she found herself looking directly at Rhulani, who was standing in the doorway to the kitchen.

"Don't worry about me, I'll manage on my own," Tondani smiled before picking up the dessert tray and walking past Rhulani out of the kitchen.

Zandi wanted to leave as well, to get away from him, but she was transfixed. She decided it wasn't her; it was his intense look that made it impossible for her to move. This look was piercing her, going right to her core, taking control of her emotions and stirring them around until she wasn't sure what it was she was supposed to be feeling at that moment. Her kitchen was generally warmer than the rest of the flat, but she was sure the heat she was feeling all of a sudden had nothing to do with the temperature.

Zandi quickly turned away from Rhulani, aware of the fact that he was moving; the distance between them was getting smaller and her emotions were being stirred at such a fast pace that she could hardly focus. Then his hand was on hers and the loss of focus ended; she couldn't have been more aware of what was happening to her. Rhulani's hand started moving slowly upwards over her arm and she knew there was no other hand she would rather have touching her right now. No other hand she would rather have move slowly over her bare shoulders and over her dress down her spine until it rested on her waist, giving her goose bumps.

Zandi knew she should be afraid. She loved everything she was feeling; she loved to have goose bumps all over. She was allowing Rhulani's hands on either side of her waist to slowly turn her around. He was looking as tempting as dark chocolate and his lips were almost on hers. She felt as if she didn't have the strength to push him away.

But at that moment she remembered all the horrible things he had said to her on that fateful date, and how she'd felt when he invited her for lunch and made her cook. She wanted this kiss, she needed it – but she needed much more to feel loved, cared for, cherished and special. That was what she deserved.

Zandi broke free of Rhulani's embrace and rushed out of the kitchen.

She was pleased to see the strawberry ice cream on the table when she got back to where the guests were having dessert. Zandi took a large spoonful of it; she needed to cool down.

"I was worried you'd miss my speciality," Simphiwe grinned at Zandi, obviously proud of the ice cream he'd made. It had a smooth texture and contained thin slices of strawberries.

"I had something to take care of. This is really, really good!"

"The guy who was sitting on your other side has also been gone for a while. His ice cream is starting to melt and I'm afraid that spoils it."

"Oh, he's not an ice cream person." Zandi saw Simphiwe's eyes widen at her comment and wished she'd kept quiet.

Rhulani came back and took his seat, only to be offered ice cream immediately by Simphiwe. "You need to eat it before it melts, otherwise it's not as good."

"I really am not an ice cream person," Rhulani said politely, while Zandi just stuffed another spoonful into her mouth. She could see Simphiwe putting the pieces together and realised that now was probably not a good time to ask him to be her date at the wedding.

After dessert people started to leave, and Zandi realised that Rhulani had also left without saying another word to her. She decided it would do her good to start cleaning up in the kitchen; maybe that would clear her head a bit.

Tondani joined her shortly afterwards. "Tonight went well," she said, and Zandi nodded. It had gone well in that no one had set her place on fire or thrown up on her carpet, but she still didn't have a date. On top of that she'd been made aware that her feelings for Rhulani were still very much alive and hard to ignore. Because of that, she was going to try her best to avoid the cause of such feelings resurfacing – being around him.

"So what's up?" her friend asked. "Do you have a date?"

Zandi rolled her eyes. "The kind of man I'm looking for doesn't exist. I've made my peace with it; I'm going to the wedding alone."

"What's wrong with Simphiwe?"

"Nothing. But Rhulani spoiled it for me. Simphiwe went

away thinking he and I are a couple. I don't know why you had to invite Rhulani."

Neo walked into the kitchen and closed the door behind her with a big sigh. "The last of the guests have left! Thanks for organising everything, you guys. Thabo and I really appreciate it."

"We're glad you enjoyed the dinner; at least that's one thing that went well tonight." Tondani threw her hands in the air. "Zandi still doesn't have a date. All those single men, and she couldn't ask even one."

"Why don't you ask Rhulani?" Neo suggested. "It's just a few hours, and then you never have to see him again if you don't want to."

"You don't know what happened when Rhulani invited me to his place for lunch," Zandi countered. "I went there expecting a meal cooked by him and then ended up having to do it myself. I've never been so shocked in my life!"

"Are you serious? This is incredibly funny!" Tondani managed to gasp before both she and Neo started laughing hysterically.

Zandi suddenly saw the humour in it as well. How could that have happened to her? "It's funny now, but believe me, it wasn't when it happened. He really didn't see anything wrong with suggesting that I make us lunch."

"That guy is as romantic as the man who gave Neo back the card, that she'd given him for his birthday, on their anniversary." Tondani couldn't help but bring that up. They always had a good laugh whenever they recalled that incident. Even Zandi thought the scene with Rhulani was nothing compared to what had happened to Neo.

"That's the reason I can't be around Rhulani any more."

Tondani made a great show of clearing her throat. "Okay, Miss I-can't-be-around-Rhulani-any-more, would you care to tell us how long you were in here with the aforesaid gentleman? And maybe while you're at it, expand a little on what the two of you were doing?"

Zandi grinned and quickly covered her face with one hand. "I can't say, but I must admit that I do have feelings for Rhulani. My heart somersaults whenever he smiles at me or touches me." She uncovered her face, saw Tondani and Neo smiling widely and continued, "But that just means that I'm still recovering from my break-up; I'm vulnerable right now."

"I'm simply going to say it the way it is: that's a lame excuse. You're crazy about Rhulani. I've watched you together, and it's so obvious!" Tondani said.

"Okay, so I'm crazy about a man who's obviously crazy, judging from our lunch date at his place. That makes me crazier than I already thought I was. But I'm not crazy enough to let this craziness go on."

"I'm going to leave now; Thabo is waiting for me outside. Good luck, because you're stuck in here with a crazy woman," Neo said to Tondani and quickly left the kitchen.

There were a few moments of silence, then Tondani said, "Maybe Rhulani is your soul mate. You'll never know if you guys don't give each other a chance."

"You don't know him the way I do. Rhulani's only soul mate is Rhulani. There's no space for me in his heart."

"Okay, let's leave the soul mate issue alone. Just ask him if he'd go to the wedding with you."

"No, I'm going alone. Even though I can already hear the women from Neo's mother's stokvel gossiping: 'Shame, look at her wearing that expensive dress! She's trying to make up for her lack of a man.'"

Tondani was laughing uncontrollably. "I'm glad you can joke about it."

Zandi was surprised when the doorbell rang early on Thursday morning. She wondered if her dinner guests had made too much noise the previous night. Had her neighbours complained and was she now about to be served with a warning? The last person she expected to find at her door was Rhulani.

"Hi."

"Hi. I'm so sorry to drop in like this. Your phone just kept on ringing and I really need the jacket today," Rhulani said, still standing outside the door. Zandi didn't know what he was talking about.

"The jacket?"

"Yes, I forgot my jacket on your balcony last night."

"I haven't gone out there this morning, so I haven't seen anything." Zandi opened the door wider for him to come in.

"I'll quickly fetch it, if you don't mind," he said.

"Of course." Zandi watched Rhulani go through the

sliding door to the balcony. He returned holding a jacket while searching its inside pocket.

"I needed my other phone that I forgot in this pocket. See you on Saturday." Rhulani smiled at Zandi with the same kind of piercing look he had given her the previous night. She suddenly felt uncomfortable, wondering if it had anything to do with what had happened between them in her kitchen.

"Saturday?"

"Sizwe told me he's invited you to come and watch our game."

"Yes, he did. See you on Saturday." Zandi felt a little relieved as she walked Rhulani to the door. She didn't know what she would have done if she had to endure that piercing look a second longer.

Nevertheless, she was pleased that he had come by her flat. She had got a fresh view of that seductive smile, which she somehow thought looked so much better in the morning. After saying goodbye to Rhulani, Zandi walked back through her living room and revelled in the scent of his deodorant that still lingered there.

She was looking forward to Saturday.

8

It was a beautiful, warm day and Sandton was buzzing with people going about their business. Zandi wondered if the weather had anything to do with how she was feeling; she was in a much better mood than she'd been in for a long time. As she sat in the restaurant, she thought about how rough the past four months had been.

She and Jeffrey had been together since they both graduated from Wits University and he was the man she was planning to spend the rest of her life with. To her, Jeffrey had always been the sweetest, the most caring, the cleverest, the funniest, the most handsome, the strongest . . . That was why she thought she would never be able to love anyone that way again.

But then she met Rhulani and rediscovered love, except he waited until she fell for him so that he could start treating her badly. However, today Zandi was happy and relieved; a voice inside was telling her she was over Rhulani for good. She didn't sit around wondering whether or not to call him any more.

She had already concluded that what happened at Neo's pre-wedding dinner on Wednesday was due to the alcohol in the apple brandy sauce that she'd had a handsome helping of with the roast beef. If it hadn't been for that, she wouldn't have gone further than greeting Rhulani, and only because it was the civil thing to do. In addition, she had concluded that telling her friends she didn't need a date for the wedding was also due to not being able to think straight. She wasn't about to let the women from Neo's mother's stokvel have a field day with her.

Zandi was on the lookout for a date again and that gave her hope for the future. Today she smiled broadly at the waiter who brought her coffee, making a mental note to ask her friends' opinion on whether she should ask him to the wedding. He was kind of cute, maybe a little young, but definitely cute. She also wasn't really sure if the well-dressed man sitting at the table opposite her was glancing at her every thirty seconds, or if he was looking at the entrance behind her. Either way, she wasn't going to let any opportunity of meeting a potential date go past by not smiling back at him. But then a woman who was obviously late rushed in to join the man at the table. At that moment Zandi also noticed that the well-dressed man wore a wedding band. Feeling like an idiot, she decided to change chairs and sit with her back to the couple.

A few minutes later Tondani walked into the restaurant. "Sorry I'm late."

"We still have fifteen minutes before the movie starts; we can skip the trailers and wait for Neo while we're at it. Have some coffee. I hope you didn't forget the tickets."

"No, I didn't, but I forgot to tell you Neo can't make it." Tondani signalled to the waiter. The young man who had served Zandi earlier came to take her order and then walked away. "You must have been waiting long," Tondani said apologetically.

"I was starting to feel like part of the décor, being as gorgeous as I am!" Zandi joked, sipping her coffee slowly and almost kissing the edge of the cup with her pouting lips before placing it neatly on the saucer.

"I'm sure the men in the restaurant weren't complaining. You could've chatted them up." Tondani winked at Zandi.

"I could have, but I haven't dated for so long that I would probably have said the wrong things and made them run for the door. I didn't want to risk being thrown out of the restaurant because I was chasing customers away."

"You've been on a few dates with Rhulani."

"Ah, it's all so stressful," Zandi complained.

"Nonsense," Tondani said. "The possibility of new love isn't supposed to be a cause for stress; it's supposed to be exciting!"

"Rhulani doesn't count. Especially since I found out that on top of having bad manners, he's got a bad memory."

Zandi's friend raised one eyebrow and she explained. "He showed up at my place yesterday morning. He'd forgotten his jacket on my balcony."

Tondani's jaw dropped in disbelief. "And you fell for that? Come on, girlfriend! He left the jacket there on purpose!"

"Why would you say that?" Zandi was genuinely puzzled.

"I know the signs, okay. That's what someone does if he wants to see you again. They 'accidentally' leave something at your place. The man clearly has a thing for you. I can't believe how you just don't see it."

Zandi remembered the incident in her kitchen, but then she saw the waiter walking towards them with her friend's coffee and decided he was a better subject for conversation than Rhulani.

"What do you think of him?" Zandi asked, looking dreamily at the waiter. There was just something about a man handling food that she found alluring.

Tondani lunged forward so that she could look straight into Zandi's face. "Are you kidding? The guy's half your age!"

Zandi giggled as the waiter placed the coffee on the table in front of Tondani. "You know, I almost asked Modise to go to the wedding with me."

Tondani was quick to give her opinion. "Modise, your boss? Girl, you're desperate! How old is he?"

"Sixty-something, but he's a cute sixty-something," Zandi said playfully. It was true that she found Modise cute, but given the choice, she still wouldn't ask him to go to a wedding with her.

"Don't say things like that. If you go with Modise it means that I'm a very bad friend . . . You have to find a hot young man – but no younger than twenty-five – to be your partner at the wedding."

"What's wrong with dating someone under twenty-five? I'm still twenty-nine for another week, you know. Everyone's dating younger men these days."

"Everyone who's a movie star – which reminds me, if we don't leave now, we'll be late for the main show."

Zandi pushed through a row of people who were already seated in the movie theatre. She couldn't believe that Tondani had bought tickets for seats that were this far away from the aisle. But even as irritated as she was, she was doing her best not to accidentally crush anyone's toes. When they were almost at their seats, the screen went black for the movie to start. Suddenly it was dark and Zandi stepped on someone's toes: the man she was about to sit next to hadn't even bothered to move his feet under his seat.

"I'm so sorry," Zandi apologised to the dark figure sitting on her right as soon as she had settled into her seat. "Did I hurt your toes?"

"Not only my toes but my whole foot," the man said, and even before there was light from the screen Zandi knew whose voice it was.

"Rhulani? I . . . I couldn't really see where I was going. I'm terribly sorry." Zandi couldn't believe that she had come to watch a movie and then ended up sitting right next to him of all people. What were the odds of that happening? She understood that it was a Friday night and wasn't surprised that Rhulani was at the movies. But in the same theatre? Sitting right next to her?

Zandi was still puzzling about this when she realised that the man on the other side of Rhulani was Lutendo. Suddenly she understood that this was not a coincidence. The tickets had been bought with the sole purpose of getting Rhulani and her together. Neo had never been part of this outing.

Zandi considered leaving but decided against it; Rhulani wasn't worth stepping on more than ten people's toes if she were to leave. She was determined rather to keep her eyes fixed on the screen for the next ninety minutes and ignore everything to her right.

To her great dismay they were watching a romantic comedy. The girl sobbed way too much and the guy was always there to kiss her tears away. It made Zandi wish she had never agreed to the movie in the first place, and then it made her wish she had left as soon as she saw Rhulani sitting next to her.

But then she became absorbed in the movie, lost in the love story she wished was her own. It made her long for a guy who was never too far away from the one he loved. She longed to feel that closeness to someone again, to be held until she had no care in the world. But gradually she realised that she actually did not have a care in the world. She was feeling love all around her, and a wonderful warmth all the way to the core of her bones.

Her mind told her to let go as soon as she realised she and Rhulani were holding hands, but everything else in her refused to let go.

Eventually the movie ended and Zandi's fantasy was over. Reality was much colder than the warmth she was feeling. She swiftly let her hand slip away from Rhulani's. She could feel his gaze on her but chose not to look at him.

Outside the theatre she greeted Lutendo and thanked Tondani for the movie. Then she said goodbye and made her way to the car, trying not to listen to all the worrying thoughts in her head. She had been holding hands with

Rhulani and it felt like the most natural thing. Maybe she should have stayed a while and had coffee with him? There was no harm in that. But at the same time it was as if she couldn't get away from him fast enough.

Zandi got a fright when she heard Rhulani calling after her. She was almost at her car, so she kept on walking.

"Thank goodness I run faster than you walk. Are you ignoring me?"

Zandi stopped to face Rhulani. She wished she could explain to him that all she wanted was to get away from his spell because it was not good for her. She shouldn't have held his hand, because she wanted more than that, and he couldn't even make her feel appreciated.

"I just have a million things on my mind." At least she was being honest on that point.

Rhulani took her hand and stroked it gently. "Don't you sometimes wonder what happened to us?"

Zandi decided that was it! She didn't wonder what had happened to her and Rhulani. She knew exactly what had happened: she had fallen for a man who did not share her views on her role as a woman. She pulled her hand away firmly from him.

"Did you know about tonight; that I was going to be sitting right next to you?" she asked Rhulani.

"Not initially. Lutendo asked if I wanted to go to a movie and I agreed. Later on something came up and when I wanted to cancel, he told me why I couldn't. But I'm glad I came because I really enjoyed being with you in there."

I enjoyed myself too but I'm in control of my life, so too bad for you, Zandi thought. Then she said, "Yes, it was an enjoyable movie."

Rhulani stood speechless, as if he had no idea what to say. Then he stammered, "Please stay for a drink. Coffee, perhaps?"

"I'm afraid I can't. Sizwe is alone at home. I must get going." She turned around and walked to her car, taking deep breaths so that the cold evening air would help her get rid of the heat she was feeling.

Rhulani didn't move and he didn't say anything either.

Zandi drove off without another word. She could still see Rhulani in her rear-view mirror, looking like the most beautiful statue she had ever seen.

Zandi woke up and realised she had promised Sizwe to watch him play tennis against Rhulani. She started wondering why she hadn't put a stop to her brother's tennis lessons a long time ago. But then again, Sizwe enjoyed them so much that she couldn't spoil that for him.

Still, after what had happened with Rhulani last night, she wished she had an excuse to avoid going to the game.

Her brother was already in the kitchen.

"I hope you haven't changed your mind about coming to watch me play today," he said with a big smile on his face.

"No, I haven't. I'm looking forward to it."

"I'm making breakfast." Sizwe sounded very proud of himself.

Zandi took one look at the eggs he was frying in way too much oil and decided to give them a miss.

"I'm not in the mood for eggs, but thanks anyway."

"I guess I can do with the extra food," her brother replied. "I'll need the energy. Rhulani is in top form. I don't feel up to playing against him, but he says it'll be good for me to start competing instead of just practising."

Zandi just nodded. Clearly Sizwe had formed some bond with Rhulani that she hadn't managed to form. It seemed everyone else got along just fine with that man, except her. Why was that? Was she the problem? Or was the problem the way Rhulani treated her? Zandi decided whatever it was didn't matter any more, and went to get ready.

When she and Sizwe arrived at the tennis courts, they found Rhulani already there. Zandi greeted him and quickly went to sit on a bench, wanting to get away from that part of her which still missed this guy with the seductive voice.

They started playing and Zandi wondered how long a game of tennis went on for. She hoped not too long; she had just realised it wasn't going to be easy watching Rhulani flex his arms all afternoon. She now understood why they were so strong.

Zandi found the contrast between Rhulani's dark skin and his all-white outfit beautiful. He was wearing a golf shirt, shorts that ended just above the knee, and trainers. The light was playing beautifully around the white of his outfit and the glow of his skin; she couldn't keep her eyes off him.

She was distracted by her phone ringing. It was To-ndani.

"Girl, are you planning anything to celebrate your birthday next week?" Tondani asked after greeting.

Zandi couldn't think of any reason to celebrate. She had yet to find a man who would show her some appreciation, and she still didn't have a date for the wedding, which was only two weeks away. "I don't feel like partying, not at this point in my life. I'm just going to let it pass swiftly."

"Come on, you're turning thirty! We must do something."

"Like what?"

"Next week Sunday Lutendo and I are going for lunch at his parents' house. But you, Neo and I could go for drinks in the evening."

Zandi saw Tondani's unavailability as the perfect excuse not to celebrate. "Sunday evening isn't a good idea; we're all going to work the next day. I'm not even sure I want to do anything. I've got lots of work to catch up on."

"Work? On your birthday? You know what, I'll make a plan to leave right after lunch so that we can go out in the afternoon. And I'll invite some people," Tondani offered.

"No! I don't want a crowd, just the three of us."

"Should I invite Rhulani?"

Zandi looked at him flexing his arms on the tennis court and yearned to say yes but replied, "I don't think that's a good idea. He doesn't even know it's my birthday."

"I don't understand the two of you. And don't deny

that there's something going on between you and him because I was there last night; I saw it myself."

Zandi kept her eyes fixed on Rhulani and answered, "I wasn't about to deny anything."

"So? When are you going to talk to the man? Tell him how you feel about him. Tell him how his behaviour makes you feel. Sometimes people aren't aware of how their actions affect the next person."

Zandi sighed and looked into the distance. "Oh, Tondani, how is that going to help?"

"If Rhulani cares about you, which I believe he does, he won't want to carry on doing things that upset you. He won't want to keep on treating you the way you don't want to be treated. He'll try his best to put a smile on your face."

Zandi looked at him again. "I'll think about it."

The friends said their goodbyes and Zandi realised that Tondani had a point. She hadn't told Rhulani about the things that made her decide to keep her distance. Things had been good between them in the beginning, which gave her hope that he did have a good side to him. He probably just needed encouragement to show that aspect of himself more.

Zandi refocused her attention on the game but then started to wonder why she had to be the one to talk to Rhulani. She had done nothing wrong; she'd simply fallen in love with a man who turned out to be undeserving of her affection. If there was anything to be said about Rhulani's behaviour, he would have to make that call himself. Until he did that, Zandi was happy to sit on the bench and enjoy the view.

The game ended and even though Sizwe had lost, he still seemed happy with how he had improved.

"I think you did well," Zandi said to her brother, a little guilty that her eyes had not been on him for most of the game.

"I guess I was too ambitious, thinking I'd beat Rhulani. Did you see how good he is?" Sizwe said, throwing his sports bag into the boot of the car.

Zandi had tried to avoid Rhulani after the game, but now she turned around and found herself looking right into his dark eyes. "Yes, he *is* good," Zandi said, still looking into those irresistible eyes.

Rhulani looked a bit embarrassed by her compliment and did the usual thing with his lower lip. She finally tore her gaze away from him and realised that Sizwe was already sitting in the car. She closed the boot and decided they'd better get going.

"How about I take the two of you out to dinner tonight?" Rhulani said before Zandi could say goodbye.

"Sizwe has a test on Monday that he has to study for."

"Then maybe you and I could go out. Just the two of us."

Zandi took a few seconds as she considered Rhulani's suggestion. She would have liked that: having dinner with him like they had done in the beginning. But then she realised she didn't have any guarantee it would be like back then again, and she couldn't stand another one of those dinners with Rhulani that had gone all sour.

"Thanks but no thanks. I'm really busy this week."

Rhulani opened his mouth as if to say something, but then he just bit his lower lip.

Zandi said goodbye and got into her car, thinking how attractive he looked when he did that.

9

Zandi wondered whether it was because it had been a hectic week at work that time had flown by so quickly or whether the wheels of time were eager to get her to her birthday. Either way, turning thirty brought with it some kind of relief for her. Now she just had to make peace with the things she had planned to do before turning thirty but had not achieved. And her aunts had to make peace with the fact that she was still unmarried.

Jeffrey now belonged to the past, and Rhulani . . . Zandi had done all she could to sort out things between them but it was difficult, what with him not even trying to meet her halfway. How was she supposed to tell the man what she didn't like about his behaviour when he wouldn't take the first step and apologise for the way he'd treated her? Or at least ask her if there was anything wrong if he really had no clue? Zandi was thirty, and she was now wise enough to figure out that Rhulani was nothing but a waste of her time.

As she toasted her birthday with her friends, she decided to cut all ties with Rhulani. She was going to get Sizwe a new tennis coach so that she didn't even have to watch the man flex his arms on the tennis court.

"So, you're finally thirty like the rest of us. Any big plans for the future?" Tondani said, raising her glass.

"The only big plan I have is getting a date for the wedding, since it turned out it wasn't as easy as you said it would be."

"Haven't I done everything I could to help? I arranged for you to meet Rhulani. And you even met Simphiwe at the dinner the other night. You're the one who's made it difficult for yourself."

"Now that you've mentioned it, I still have Simphiwe's number. I suppose it wouldn't hurt to call and say, 'By the way, I've broken up with the guy you thought I was seeing. How about we go to the wedding together?'"

"So have things between you and Rhulani taken a different turn?" Tondani asked. "The last time I checked you were going to talk to him."

Zandi realised she didn't know how to answer her friend honestly. Even though she had decided she would give Rhulani a chance to prove himself, she wondered if she had really thought he would prove to be a different person at the end of it all. He couldn't even take the first step to make things right between them. Because the truth was, she really liked him. All she had wished for the whole week was for him to call and apologise for being such a pig. She would have told him that she thought he was way sexier than a pig, and they would have put everything behind them and moved on happily with their lives.

But when Rhulani called her, it seemed he was only doing so to castigate her for being so devoted to her work that she didn't even have time for dinner with him. That got her truly upset, and she told him that maybe if he was nicer she would have more time to speak to him, after which she slammed the phone down.

Thinking about the incident, Zandi sighed. "Rhulani's still being mean. He's got issues, and while I might have taken it in my twenties, I'm not going to put up with stuff like that any more. I've decided not to see him again."

"Way to go, sister! Let's toast to that!"

Neo and Zandi raised their glasses, but Tondani ignored them. "You're not even giving Rhulani a chance to talk to you. How is he going to do that if you won't see him?" she asked.

Zandi played with the straw in her drink. "I don't know. Maybe I want him to try harder. Like say it on a billboard that I drive past on my way to work."

"That would be so cool!" Neo nodded her head in agreement.

"It's okay to dream but you need to be realistic," Tondani warned.

Zandi didn't like her friend's tone of voice. She didn't think she was being unrealistic by deciding not to see Rhulani until he had apologised for his behaviour.

"How did the dress fitting go?" Zandi asked, changing the subject on purpose.

Neo shook her head repeatedly. "It's a disaster in the making. Thabo insisted that we use his aunt, but I doubt she's ever made anything decent before. I have a feeling it will be in the running for ugliest wedding dress ever made."

"You still have time; just change dressmakers," Zandi said jokingly.

"The wedding is a week away and that will just cost us more money. It's not like I haven't tried speaking to Thabo about this, but he checks how any new expense will affect his net worth before agreeing to something. Have you ever dated an accountant?"

Zandi and Tondani laughed as Neo took a large sip of her margarita.

"Thabo clearly has too much time on his hands. Shouldn't the two of you be checking on each other's assets, rather than checking your net assets?" Tondani chuckled.

"Neo, if you still want to get married in a week's time you really shouldn't listen to Tondani," warned Zandi. "You have enough stress as it is without her causing you any more."

"Poor me!" Tondani exclaimed dramatically. "I get blamed whenever something goes wrong; that's why I'm so glad that things are going well for everyone at the moment. Neo is getting married, so who cares what the dress looks like? And Zandi is in love with Rhulani, though she'd like us to believe she doesn't want to see him any more."

Zandi sighed, wondering if being in love with Rhulani meant anything at all right now.

Neo was at her wits' end because she couldn't see the situation with her wedding dress improving. "Zandi, why don't you just give me your wedding dress?"

Zandi didn't want to be reminded of that dress. "We've talked about this," she told her friend. "I can't let you have it." Zandi had bought the wedding dress six months before her break-up with Jeffrey because she really loved it.

The other reason she'd bought the dress was because at that point she believed that she and Jeffrey were not too far from tying the knot. She had obviously been mistaken, but she still didn't want to give the dress away. To her that felt like giving up all hope of ever getting married. Unfortunately Neo had already seen the dress and gone as far as to try it on, and even Zandi had to agree that it looked much better on her friend's curvier figure.

"Neo, you don't want to hurt Thabo's aunt's feelings by not wearing the dress she's made for you. And what's more, our birthday girl is in love, so she might be getting married sooner than we think," Tondani said and winked at Zandi.

Neo mumbled something about being the ugliest bride that ever walked down the aisle and Zandi mumbled something about not being sure about getting married any time soon.

Since Zandi was not as tipsy as Neo, Tondani could make out what she had said and promptly replied, "I can see when two people are made for each other, and you and Rhulani are a perfect match, so stop saying that."

"I know I'm pushing Rhulani away, but I want him to be the first to admit that his behaviour towards me was wrong."

"Zandi, the truth is you arc partly to blame for this sit uation you've created. If you had a problem with Rhulani, you should've spoken to him about it. You should've told him exactly what you don't like about his behaviour," Tondani maintained.

"Okay, I see your point. I guess I was just being stubborn."

Neo had calmed down a bit by now and Tondani was looking at Zandi with a smile.

"Now that we've got the serious matters out of the way . . . Here's a little something that Neo and I got you for your birthday. It's nothing big, just a symbol of our appreciation for being such a good friend." Tondani handed Zandi a small box.

"Thank you so much; I love gifts and I'm going to open it right now!" Zandi started to unwrap the box.

"It's something we thought would go really well with the dress you bought for the wedding. And we know you'll love them because we have good taste," Tondani said with a broad smile.

Zandi finished unwrapping the box and took out a pair of silver chandelier earrings. "Oh, they're so pretty, but Neo has a wedding coming up; you shouldn't have got me such an expensive gift."

Neo grinned. "You turn thirty only once and we wanted to get you something decent. That's why Tondani bought the earrings and I bought the wrapping paper."

"Now that sounds like the Neo I know!" laughed Zandi. "Wow, I love these earrings, and I love the wrapping too."

"I'm glad," Neo said. "But you guys have to excuse me now. I'm supposed to go for my last dress fitting today."

Tondani looked at her watch and gasped. "I forgot it was Sunday. Can we continue this celebration another day? As you know, I must go to bed early on a Sunday otherwise my Monday is a mess."

Zandi sighed. "I can't believe you suggested celebrating my birthday and now you're both running away from me."

"Oh, you can still say that because you've only just turned thirty. Soon you'll find out that you can't stay out so late any more," Tondani joked while they got up to leave.

As Zandi walked to her car, she decided it was worth getting over her pride and letting Rhulani know what she didn't like about his behaviour towards her. It was worth giving it a try because of the way she felt about him. If nothing came of it, then she would move on, but at least she would be able to make peace with the fact that things could never work out between them. Still, she checked her phone to make sure she had kept Simphiwe's number.

Just in case.

Zandi was surprised to find Simphiwe in her house when she got home. She hadn't seen him since the dinner at her place two weeks previously. She was also surprised at how pleased she was to see his friendly smile again.

"Did I forget you were coming?" Zandi asked after they had greeted each other. As far as she was aware, Tondani had taken all the catering ware that Simphiwe had supplied for the dinner with her that evening.

"No, you didn't forget. I wanted it to be a surprise," Simphiwe said and Zandi suddenly felt uncomfortable. She wondered if this was Tondani's attempt to help her get a date for the wedding.

"Have you been waiting long?" Zandi was confused, not knowing what else to say.

Simphiwe hesitated and then answered, "Not too long. And Sizwe sat here with me until he told me you were very strict about him not watching too much TV and went to his room."

Zandi managed a sigh. "I'm sure he made it sound like I was a sister from hell, but I just want him to focus on his schoolwork, that's all."

Simphiwe smiled. "I think you're doing a great job."

Zandi's heart leaped. It felt good to be appreciated.

After an awkward silence she said, "Can I offer you something to drink?" while already making her way to the kitchen.

"Thanks, that would be nice."

The moment Zandi opened the door, a crowd in the kitchen chorused, "Surprise!"

It felt as if she had suddenly walked into a dream. Within seconds Zandi's friends were all around her, wishing her well on her birthday. Amidst all the shouting and laughing, she was trying hard to work out how this had happened without her ever suspecting a thing. Who had organised the surprise party? If it had been Neo and Tondani, she would have found out long before, because both of them were hopeless at keeping a secret.

As if on cue, the two of them came walking towards her.

"How did you guys get here so quickly? Neo was supposed to go for her dress fitting and Tondani . . ." Zandi was still trying to figure out what exactly was happening around her.

"Well, there *was* no dress fitting, and Tondani drives like a maniac. I recited my wedding vows in the car, just in case I didn't get here alive. I've waited so long to say 'I do', and then this woman tries to kill me a week before my big day!" Neo placed her hand flat on her chest as if to calm her heartbeat.

"Please keep your voice down. My mother-in-law already thinks I'm trying to kill her because she choked on the dessert I brought for lunch," Tondani said, and then turned to Zandi. "So, what do you think of the party?"

"I never suspected a thing! I'm still trying to get over the shock. How did you guys manage to organise everything without me ever being suspicious?"

"It was a combined effort with someone whose identity we can't divulge yet. We were sworn to secrecy, so we couldn't really warn you." Tondani was clearly proud that she had managed to keep mum for this long.

"Why did this secret person go through the trouble of organising all this?" Zandi asked.

"Maybe because this secret person has a thing for you. Maybe because this person's heart palpitates whenever you're near." Tondani winked and Neo giggled.

Zandi didn't like this confusion. Why couldn't they just tell her who the person was? She sighed and then noticed Simphiwe walking towards them. Tondani saw him too; she grabbed Neo by the arm and pulled her away into the crowd.

"Enjoying the party?" Simphiwe asked Zandi when he finally stood beside her.

"I am, thank you."

"I hope you'll enjoy the food too. It's with best wishes from the chef. Happy birthday." Simphiwe gave her a friendly nod and then walked away.

Zandi was more confused than ever; she still had no clue who had organised the party for her. She noticed Sizwe for the first time when he came over to her.

"Happy birthday, sis," he said, hugging her.

"Thanks, Sizwe. I love the music."

"I'm glad; that was my department," her brother said proudly. Zandi was impressed with him for knowing what kind of music she liked without her telling him. Not even Jeffrey had known her that well after all those years of dating.

Zandi decided she had figured out who the person behind the surprise party was. "How did you manage to get all of this together?" she asked Sizwe.

"I'd like to take the credit, but Rhulani did most of the work. All I did was put the music together."

"Is he here?" gasped Zandi.

Sizwe nodded towards where Rhulani was standing. It hadn't even occurred to Zandi that he was there. She looked in that direction and saw him talking to some other guy. Looking at him now, she wondered what it was about Rhulani that evoked such pulse-quickening currents within her.

At that moment he looked at her and their eyes met. Zandi suddenly felt as if the current created by her fast heartbeat was about to topple her over. She could feel the storm building up too quickly for her to try and stop it. It was a brief storm but when it was over, the unmistakable fire that she had been trying so hard to put out in the past week was burning stronger than ever before.

She forced herself to tear her gaze away from Rhulani, but her heart continued to beat wildly. Zandi decided she was more shocked than anything else. She turned her attention back to her brother.

"Are you serious? Rhulani organised all this?"

Sizwe nodded.

Zandi was still grappling with her astonishment when Tondani suddenly reappeared from the crowd. "Excuse me, can I steal her for a moment?" Tondani was already holding Zandi by the arm.

"No problem," Sizwe said and walked away.

"Girlfriend, there is something very important you need to know."

Zandi could see that Tondani was excited by whatever it was she had to tell her.

"I already know that it was Rhulani who organised the party, but that doesn't make up for everything I'm upset with him about. He and I still need to talk."

"I understand that, and that's something between the two of you. But I have another piece of information for you: earthshaking kind of info. Remember you asked me to do a background check on Rhulani when you still thought he was a serial killer? Well, I asked a friend to do it and then forgot about it because she took so long. But a few minutes ago she called me to say she had emailed the information on him. Being me, I obviously had to check straightaway in case I was actually rubbing shoulders with a wanted criminal. Anyway, it turns out that Rhulani is – "

Zandi was eagerly waiting for her friend to finish her sentence when the man himself appeared.

"Hi there," Rhulani greeted the ladies.

"I'm going to leave you two alone." Tondani walked away, leaving Zandi in a state of confusion. It seemed anyone who tried to tell her anything was interrupted.

"Happy birthday," Rhulani said and smiled at Zandi. "Are you enjoying the party?"

"Yes, thanks, it's great. Thank you for organising it. This might be my best birthday so far."

All he said was, "I'm glad."

Zandi wished she could figure out why Rhulani had gone to so much trouble to organise everything. Then she decided it was best to ask him, rather than racking her brain to find answers. "How did you know about my birthday? And why go to all this trouble?"

"Sizwe told me it was your thirtieth. He wanted to do something special for you and asked my advice. And of course I also wanted to do something special for you because I care about you so much. There were times when I've tried to stay away from you, but I've come to realise that I actually can't."

Zandi was transfixed. She could feel tears forming in her eyes because she had never heard Rhulani say anything like this to her. She had almost come to believe that he didn't care about anyone but himself, because that was what it looked like most of the time.

"I . . . I'm confused . . . You've acted very strangely towards me at times."

Rhulani took Zandi's hand and squeezed it. Then he led her to one of the bar stools and sat her down.

"There's something I need to tell you. It might help to explain some of the questions you had about my behaviour. At the same time it might help you see what an idiot I am."

Zandi was starting to feel nervous, but she managed a smile.

"As you already know, I am Rhulani Mhinga. What I haven't told you yet is that my father is the chief of Mhinga, a village in Limpopo. I am his eldest surviving son and as such I'm set to be his successor." Rhulani paused for a few moments, but his eyes kept holding Zandi's.

"When I met you . . . after I'd got to know you, I realised that I had very deep feelings for you. At that point it also struck me that it was time to find someone fit to be my queen. I admit that I went about it the wrong way, what with that stupid test of mine, and I was an idiot. I also admit that at times my pride got in the way of us being together. I should've apologised to you earlier for treating you the way I did."

Zandi was confused. "It was a test?"

"Yes, a very silly test. I wanted to see how you'd feel if you got married and were asked to quit your job, stay at home, look after your family, cook for your husband . . . Like I said, it was a silly test and it backfired. I should've known it would only push you away," Rhulani answered honestly.

"Do all those things come with dating a future chief?" Zandi asked, and he shook his head.

"Then why couldn't you just tell me that you're going to be a chief?" Zandi didn't understand why he had come up with some silly test that did nothing but drive them apart.

Rhulani looked embarrassed, doing the thing with his lower lip again. "Love makes me do silly things."

To Zandi that was the most romantic thing she'd ever heard. She could hardly believe that Rhulani had turned out to be someone who was obviously so in love with her and cared for her so deeply that he surprised her with a party on the birthday she hadn't even told him about. Just that morning she had still thought that he didn't care two hoots about her.

"It wasn't easy for me, but I couldn't put up with how you were treating me. I need a good man in my life," Zandi said, wanting to make sure that Rhulani understood what she required of him if they were to get along.

He gave her hand that he'd been holding the whole time another gentle squeeze. "You deserve a good man. If you'd like us to start over, I'd love you to get to know the good Rhulani."

Zandi realised this was the man she had fallen in love with in the beginning, the man she had been wishing would come back.

"I'd love that," she said softly and then added, "as long as you promise not to talk about business strategies for a while."

Rhulani twisted his lips as if in thought. "I'll try."

"No, you need to promise. I've heard enough to last me a few weeks, or make that a few months."

"Okay, I promise."

Rhulani helped Zandi down from the bar stool so that she was standing next to him. They forgot that they were in a room full of people; it was as if it was only the two of them. Zandi was aware of Ringo's mesmerising voice singing *Sondela* in the background and she knew that Rhulani was too. She moved closer to him and he put his arms around her, and it was as if he couldn't stop smiling at her, even if he tried.

He lowered his head and pressed his lips to hers and Zandi felt as if she was going to lose her breath. It was as if all her other senses had momentarily shut down and the only thing she was able to do was taste his kiss. It was a taste she knew would always linger on her lips.

When they finally let go of each other, Zandi and Rhulani realised for the first time that the room was echoing with oohs and aahs, while Ringo was still singing the soundtrack to their kiss.

"I've never kissed in a place full of people before," Zandi whispered.

"Neither have I." Rhulani put his arm around Zandi and held her to him.

10

Eventually the last of the guests at Zandi's surprise party left. She was pleased that it was finally just her and Rhulani. She was so glad the events of the last five hours had played out as they did; even cleaning up her place didn't seem like such a horrible job right now.

"Are you sure a chief of Mhinga is allowed to clean up after other people?" Zandi teased.

"Yes, a chief should do that. It's called leading by example."

"How do you feel about such a responsibility?"

"Apart from the fact that my father will leave really big shoes to fill?" Rhulani raised both his shoulders and then let them drop. "I'll have to make some sacrifices, like the job that I'm not allowed to talk about."

"I don't see why you can't continue doing your job. There must be businesses in your village that could benefit from your expertise. Sometimes it's much more rewarding to help small firms and see them grow."

Rhulani nodded. "I never thought of that. Now that you've mentioned it, I'm sure we could do with an economist as well."

"What do you mean?"

Rhulani tied the last of the black bags and took Zandi's

hand in his. "Do you remember earlier when you said I'm not a chief yet? That's true, but I'd like you to be by my side all the way, until I do become one."

Zandi wondered if she'd had too much to drink; she was sure she misunderstood Rhulani. "Don't you think it's too early to be saying that?"

"My father is a very wise man, as you can imagine. He once told me that I'd know when I've found the one to spend the rest of my life with. Right now, standing here beside you, I know you are that person. I love you, Zandi." Rhulani said the words so lovingly that she felt enveloped by his love.

"I love you too," Zandi said, momentarily feeling over-whelmed by her feelings for this man.

Rhulani took her in his arms and held her; she felt warm and relaxed.

But something still bothered her and she knew she had to address it. "Earlier you said a woman should quit her job, look after the family and cook for the husband . . . Is that something that comes with being married to the chief of Mhinga?"

"Initially that's what I thought," Rhulani answered. "But it turns out you don't have to do any of those things. You certainly don't have to quit your job. You can look after the family but you can get help if needed. Cooking for the husband is completely optional. If he's an idiot like me, you can feed him uncooked food and he won't know the difference."

As Zandi laughed at what Rhulani had said, she realised

how much she had missed his sense of humour. Then something else came to her mind and she suddenly stopped laughing.

"Since you're going to be a chief, how many children are you expected to have?" she asked nervously.

"Are you worried because you don't want any?"

"It's not that I don't want children. It's just that I dated a man who really didn't like kids and I started to see them through his eyes. But that isn't what I want for myself. I'd love to have children, though I couldn't manage thirty." Zandi sighed, happy that she had got that out of the way.

Rhulani understood the true reason for her concern. "I don't want thirty children, and I want to marry only one woman."

"Isn't it expected of you to have many wives and many kids?" Zandi blinked, feeling a little silly. She couldn't believe she was interrogating him about how many children he wanted and the number of wives he was planning to marry. But she had to know those details before making any kind of commitment to him.

"Some people still expect it, but others have accepted that times have changed. Luckily my father is one such man, and as long as he is on my side, I trust his wisdom to make people see that there's nothing wrong about a chief marrying only one wife."

"Wow, I wish I knew someone with such wisdom."

"You will, soon."

Zandi felt a flush of warmth go through her veins. But the thought of meeting the wise chief of Mhinga also made her feel a bit nervous. She smiled at Rhulani and decided to rather focus on what was happening at that moment. She enjoyed rinsing the glasses after he'd washed them. She liked this new Rhulani so much more.

By the time everything was clean and packed away, Zandi was so exhausted that she didn't think she could stand on her feet much longer. She and Rhulani went to the lounge and collapsed on the couch.

"You know, it's almost two and I'm supposed to be at work at half past eight in the morning," Zandi said, laughing at how tired she was.

"Are you joking? It was your birthday and you've just had a party to celebrate. Surely you're allowed a day off to recover? I know I'm taking today off." Rhulani played with Zandi's braids.

"Was it your birthday as well?" Zandi asked jokingly.

"I have a better excuse; it was my girlfriend's birthday." Rhulani kissed Zandi on the cheek and she giggled.

"It's easier for you to stay away from work. You're your own boss. I hate to let Modise down."

"You're not handing in your resignation; you're just taking a day off." Rhulani raised his eyebrows. "Do you know you need to take leave regularly to be a productive employee?"

Zandi realised she couldn't even remember when last she'd taken a break. "Well then, I must've stopped being productive at work a long time ago, and that's not sitting well with me right now. But what's the point of taking a day off if I must still take Sizwe to school?"

"Your brother has agreed that you won't be in any state to drive anyone anywhere in the morning. I've already asked his friend's mother to give him a lift to school."

Zandi puckered her lips and then smiled. "I see you've thought of everything. I'll call Modise at eight."

"Does that mean I can sleep over?" Rhulani asked, but regretted asking when he saw the look on Zandi's face. She was obviously not ready for him to do that.

"Cancel that, I didn't mean it. I really should be going. You've had a long day; I'm sure you'd like a rest." Rhulani kissed Zandi gently before getting up to leave.

She got up with him. "Wait, I want to ask you something. Would you like to come with me to Neo's wedding? It's only a week away."

"I'd love to. We'll discuss the details later; get some rest."

"Hang on, there's one more thing. Please wait here; I won't be long."

Zandi rushed off to her room and left a puzzled Rhulani standing in the middle of her lounge. When she returned, she was holding the suit she had bought the day she got her dress for the wedding. She handed it to him.

"You're giving me a suit?" Rhulani was now even more perplexed.

"It goes with the dress I'll be wearing to the wedding. I'd like you to try it on. I'll leave you to change; call me when you're done."

Zandi went to her room, somehow feeling silly about what she was doing. But then she remembered Tondani's words about being in control of her life and didn't feel silly any more. Now she just felt nervous about the possibility of the suit not fitting Rhulani. Zandi had kept it because she believed that when she found the man she was meant to be with, the suit would fit him. Right now she believed Rhulani was that man; she had no doubts about that. But what if the suit didn't fit him? Would that make her doubt that he was the man for her?

As Rhulani knocked on Zandi's door, she decided that this was really a silly test. Whether he fitted into the suit had nothing to do with her love for him.

She went and opened the door, and when she saw Rhulani in the suit he was looking more handsome than she had ever seen him.

"It fits you," Zandi said, almost not believing her own words.

"Yes, it does – perfectly."

Rhulani was as surprised as he was impressed. "How did you know it would fit me?"

"I knew because you're the man I've been dreaming about all my life."

Zandi could not help but gasp at how striking Rhulani looked. She had imagined what her date would look like in the suit, but the picture hadn't been nearly as good as what she was seeing in front of her.

He grinned. "I must admit, out of all the suits I own, I don't have one that fits me this well. I'm stunned." Rhulani took Zandi's hand and pulled her closer to him.

"You look rather irresistible in this," she said as she adjusted the tie and the collar of the shirt.

Rhulani twisted his lips seductively. "It does enhance how irresistible I am, doesn't it? But I can assure you, what's underneath is even more irresistible."

Zandi smiled at his joke and said, "I think you need to take off the suit before it gets creased." She was aware of Rhulani's hands firmly around her waist, holding her close to him as if he was never going to let go.

He pulled her closer and gave her a slow, lingering kiss. She could feel her heart race, clearly overwhelmed by all the things she was feeling from his closeness. The layers of the suit started coming off one by one, and neither of them cared that the clothes were dropping on the floor at their feet. Zandi marvelled at the feel of Rhulani's warm skin and how it gleamed in the light like delectable dark chocolate.

"Wait, I'm Zulu," she managed to whisper.

"Really? I wouldn't have guessed, but thanks for sharing." Rhulani smiled before starting to kiss Zandi again.

"You don't get it. I'm Zulu; you're Tsonga. The people from your village will expect you to marry a Tsonga girl." Zandi was breathing heavily. The last thing she wanted to think about now was that something could stand in the way of her and Rhulani being together, but at the same time she couldn't ignore this.

"Not the last time I checked. My father's wives aren't all Tsonga, and no one treats them differently from the local wives."

"As easy as that?" Zandi wanted to say. But it seemed at that moment Rhulani preferred her lips to be on his and not talking to him, so she resorted to keeping her thoughts to herself. She could feel herself falling under his spell, and she wanted to hold back, to grasp at anything that might steady her and prevent her from falling for him so fast. The best she could manage was to grasp at the million thoughts going around in her mind.

This man she was with at three in the morning was a future chief of a tribe in a village she had never been to. A tribe that was different from hers, and most probably had different customs. How would she survive in that village, as the chief's wife? Surely people would expect her at least to be able to speak their language and know their culture? Zandi was getting overwhelmed with what was going on in her mind and what Rhulani was doing to her body. With each passing moment and each slight increase in heart rate, what she was feeling throughout her body was starting to make her lose control of her thoughts.

"I can't . . . I can't speak Xitsonga," Zandi gasped.

Rhulani chuckled. "I'll teach you."

She relaxed. The way Rhulani held her, Zandi felt she could trust this man and love him without holding back. And how could she hold back when just his warm breath on her skin had the ability to melt her to the core of her bones? She suddenly felt no need to grasp at anything any more and the million thoughts in her mind vanished. They couldn't withstand the soft kisses that sent shivers throughout her body. Zandi was completely under Rhulani's spell and ready to learn everything he could teach her about love.

Zandi stretched and yawned, looking at her cellphone that kept on ringing. She wondered if it would ever stop, but she knew Tondani wasn't going to give up that easily, and finally answered.

"Hello?"

"Girlfriend, your secretary said you called to say you were taking the day off." Tondani sounded worried.

"Yes, I'm still in bed," Zandi answered sheepishly.

"Are you all right? I hope you didn't drink too much after we left."

Zandi remembered everything that happened after her friends had left and smiled to herself, glad that she had been sober throughout.

"No, I'm fine. I just needed the rest, that's all."

Tondani gasped, much too loudly. "Is it what I'm thinking? Is there a man in your room right now?"

"No, there's no man in my room. But there's a man in my house." Zandi giggled and could imagine the look on Tondani's face as she chuckled on the other end.

"Did Rhulani sleep over, or did he just decide to come by your place to say good morning?"

"That's none of your business," Zandi said and giggled again.

Tondani gave up trying to get information out of her friend. "Be glad that you've turned thirty, because I was going to come to your place right now and demand an explanation for your behaviour – and his."

"I'm so glad I'm thirty!"

"What is this I hear about you giving your wedding

dress to Neo? I would've understood that a week ago, but now you have a man."

"I did call Neo earlier to tell her she could have the dress. Mine will be a traditional Tsonga wedding, and fortunately I don't need curves to look good in a xibelani."

"Come to think of it, you'd look gorgeous wearing a xibelani. I must find out if we can get you a designer one; this is so exciting!" Tondani exclaimed.

"A designer xibelani? You know what, I'm getting off the phone right now. Bye!" Zandi hung up as Rhulani walked in with a breakfast tray. He was wearing an apron, and on it he had written with a red permanent marker:

Joburg's finest chef

Zandi couldn't stop giggling; she had waited for this moment for too long. "Does the 'finest' refer to the food or the chef himself?"

"Lucky for you, it refers to both." Rhulani placed the tray next to her.

Zandi was impressed by the effort she could see he had put into making the breakfast. Her coffee mug had a pink ribbon around it, tied into a cute bow. The scrambled eggs were served in a heart shape on the plate. There were slices of toast and a bowl of fruit salad with yoghurt spooned onto the top in a heart shape.

"Did you really make this all by yourself?"

Rhulani nodded. "Of course. You really have the wrong impression of me."

Zandi frowned playfully. "Are you surprised?"

"That wasn't me. The real Rhulani will be making you lunch and then supper. The real Rhulani thinks you're a truly amazing sister, daughter and employee . . . I guess what I'm trying to say is that you're a truly amazing woman," he said while giving her soft kisses on her cheeks.

"I think I'm amazing too," Zandi teased and then said, "What's with all these heart shapes?"

"I suppose it's true what they say: when you're in love it shows in everything you do."

"I also believe that action speaks louder than words," Zandi grinned as she reached for Rhulani's apron strings.

They had the whole morning to finish breakfast.

TSIRE MUSHOMA grew up in Venda in the Limpopo Province and currently resides in Johannesburg. One of her Tshivenda short stories was included in the POWA Women's Writing Anthology in 2005 and another was included in the same anthology in 2006. Her English short story "A new beginning" was awarded fourth place in the 2007 BTA/Anglo Platinum Short Story Writing Competition. *Nne na Inwi* was published by Tafelberg Publishers in 2008. *The Bridesmaid's Lover* is her second novel.

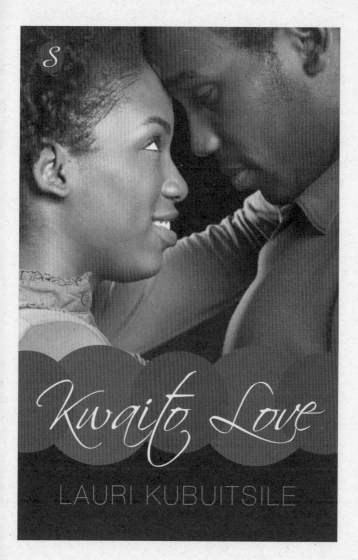

Kwaito Love

LAURI KUBUITSILE

Cherry Marbles

SHUKIE NKOSANA

Where true love reigns

Sapphire
PRESS

Are you a writer? Do you want to get published?
Write a truly South African romance novel for
our new romance imprint, Sapphire Press – only
30 000 words. Email sapphire@kwela.com for
more information, or to let us know if you liked
this story. Alternatively, send us a letter to Kwela
Books, PO Box 6525, Roggebaai, 8012. You can
also fax us at 021 406 3812. Feedback will be
given on publishable manuscripts only.